I0576078

DRAGON'S TREASURE

ADDISON JAMES

ADDISON JAMES

To Nana--

You would have hated everything about this book except the fact that I had written it. Thank you for always encouraging me. I wish you were here to see this.

CONTENTS

CONTENT NOTES

*Unequal power dynamics (royalty/servant)

    *Imprisonment

    *Threats of violence/harm

    *On page fighting/violence

    *18+ sexual scenes

CHAPTER ONE

LEANA

The days where I go to the prison are always long days.

I wake up before dawn, carefully creeping out of the room I share with three other girls. They don't have much longer to sleep before their own days begin, but I don't want to take away a single moment of sleep. It's always so precious to us, especially recently. There's been a lot of long days lately, what with dragons all over the kingdom taking up residence in the palace.

From there, I need to requisition my supply bag. It would be much easier if I could go and simply fill it in the kitchen, but instead, a soldier has to personally hand me a bag. It doesn't matter that he did exactly what I would do. It doesn't matter that the king is chained, far beneath the ground, and hasn't moved in a century. His imprisonment is apparently still a matter the military gets involved in.

I don't argue. Four years in and everything is routine, but even when this first started, I didn't argue. This isn't the type of place where arguing is rewarded, and I learned my place a long time ago.

From there, a different soldier—this one a dragon—hands me the key to the grate at the top of the cave. I tuck it under my tunic.

The sun is just barely breaking the horizon when I set out for the day, preparing myself for the hour-long walk. At least the path is smooth, but the pack cutting into my shoulders somehow seems heavier each week.

At last I arrive, finding myself in a rocky hillside entirely barren except for two things: a crumbling cottage, and the obvious metal grate.

The grate takes some nudging to open, but I finally prop it open and slip through, careful of my footing as I step onto the narrow, winding path.

Someone took the time to cut a path into the rocks, but they clearly didn't worry about safety. I center the pack on my back, lest its weight pull me over the edge, and begin to carefully make my way down.

All too soon, the limited light that filters in through the grate disappears. The shadows seem to multiply, reaching out to consume everything, swallowing it all for this forgotten, miserable pit.

I call the flames to my hand, lighting my way. I won't be swallowed by the darkness, at least.

This is why the prince trusts me with this task. The dark, deep prison might cut the former king off from the outside world, but I will always be able to find my way out.

I let the flames move to my upper arms when I need to use a rope, hand-over-hand, to climb down from one ledge to the next. When I'm finally on my feet again, I allow myself a break.

But only a short one. I don't have all day to finish this task, and I'll be expected back at the castle soon enough.

Finally, I make it to the base of the cave. I'm so deep that I can look up and not see the entrance. Not even a single speck of light makes it this deep.

It seems like a cruel and unusual punishment. But then again, I'm told that this is a king who did cruel and unusual things.

That little reminder worked my first few weekly visits. It sounds far less sure in my head now.

There's one last corner to turn, and then I'm facing the king.

King Osir, former ruler of the kingdom, locked up a century ago, looms over the space like some sort of underground mountain, and when I raise my hand, his red scales flicker to look like fire. He holds himself perfectly still, as if trying to blend into the rocky walls of his cave. Even so, his limbs ripple with power.

That used to be enough to remind me that he could kill me. One claw, one tooth, one squeeze of that powerful arm would be the end of me. Being able to survive his fire was no excuse to be lulled into a false sense of security.

I still know he can kill me. I can't forget it around any dragon. But now, after four years, I see more than just his looming size.

The horns on his head fade from red to gold, and I can never quite forget the crown he lost. And his eyes, pitch black and ever-watching, never truly look menacing anymore. They just look intelligent.

I bow. Whether he has a crown of jewels or a crown of his own horns hardly matters; he's a king.

"Your majesty."

Then he does what he always does, what has confused me since the beginning: he bows back.

Kings don't bow to servants. But Osir always makes sure to acknowledge me.

"Leana," he rumbles, and just that is enough to send shivers down my spine.

Chapter Two

OSIR

I'm sure when my brother locked me in this cell, he had much more devious plans for torture than boredom.

He's creative, my brother.

But boredom has been my worst enemy. For one hundred years, I have been in this hole in the earth, deprived of the sky and my throne and most basic comforts. Torturers have come and gone, but I have forgotten almost all of them, as the kingdom seems to have forgotten about me.

It might be a crueler punishment than all the torturers combined could devise.

Kings aren't meant for cages. Dragons aren't meant to be cut off from the sky. Yet here I sit.

***

The clanging of the grate lets me know my only visitor will be here shortly.

Shortly being a relative term. I don't have a good grasp on time all the way down here in the dark. But I did count one day, measuring every second between when I heard the grate and when I finally saw my beautiful treasure. It's a treacherous journey, she tells me, mostly in the dark, with winding, twisted paths built into the sheer sides of the rocks. At several points, the path down becomes so steep she's forced to use ropes to climb.

It's a shame she doesn't have a dragon to fly her out of this hellhole. I would lift her in one scaly hand, and we'd be out of here in mere minutes, with no chance of her falling down a cliff and breaking a leg, or worse.

But I'm trapped down here, left to wait for my treasure to find her slow, meticulous way to me.

She has made the journey two hundred fourteen times and has arrived with what she promised me were minor injuries only twice. She has never been more seriously injured. I just have to hope that today is not the day where that changes.

I have no grasp on day or night, here in the deep earth, so I have no way to know how long anything might take. But she tells me she comes by once a week.

So I wait patiently, day in and day out, trapped down here in the dark, for my greatest treasure to come to me.

At long last her footsteps echo closer, and she creeps into the cavern I have not left for a century. She holds one hand up, flames bursting from her skin, sending sharp, dancing shadows across her soft features.

A rumble stirs deep within me at the mere sight of her, the low sound reverberating through the stones surrounding us.

I can't help it. Dragons rumble for our mates. And just because I am currently no fit mate for Leana doesn't mean my instincts can be silenced.

Leana comes to a stop and sets her heavy pack on the ground, then bows low. "Your majesty."

"Leana." I dip my head in turn, although I always worry the gesture seems more menacing than proper. But she's never reacted poorly, and if my Leana is courteous enough to bow to a disgraced, imprisoned king, then I will certainly show the same courtesy back to her.

She straightens and moves around the cavern with measured, even steps, lighting torches with a flick of her wrist as she goes. I blink, letting my eyes adjust to the light I so rarely see.

I could blow fire if I ever desired light, but there is nothing to see down here, except for these once a week visits from Leana.

The flickering torches bring me the sight I spend my weeks dreaming about. She's a small creature, but sturdily

7

built, strong from work. Her face is soft, rounded, and the few times I've truly seen her smile have illuminated my cave better than any torch.

Her hair, black as the midnight sky, is swept back in a plain braid down her back. Practical for traipsing down to my cell, perhaps, but disappointing to see such a treasure without a single jewel to mark her status. She should have hair combs made of gold and rubies, like the flames under her skin, or maybe silver and diamonds to look like stars in her midnight hair.

Likewise, the rest of her is unadorned. Not a single piece of jewelry on her beautiful body. Not even fine cloth for her clothes. I grant that her trousers and tunic are practical for journeying down here, but dragons do not care much for practicality.

I tried once to tell her where I hid some of my hoard so she could have the adornments she deserves. She had gently reminded me she was a servant, and had no use for jewels, and when I'd protested too much, she'd become quiet and withdrawn for the rest of her time with me. I'd learned my lesson, and hadn't brought it up again, even if I can't stop thinking about it.

She summons the flames to her skin one more time to light the final torch, studying her work critically. "I'll requisition more torches, your majesty. I doubt these ones will last much longer."

"Thank you, Leana." I really don't care about the torches that only get lit once a week, but I suppose if they burned down entirely, I'd have a difficult time seeing her, and that is untenable.

"Of course, your majesty. Is there anything else I should ask for on your behalf?"

She always asks, and I always decline. She would not be able to bring me anything useful. And the only thing I truly want is more time with her, but I would never condemn her to more time in this dark pit. The hour or so of her company and the supply of food will have to be enough.

She opens her pack and empties it closer to me. It must weigh nearly as much as her, but my treasure carries the week's worth of food with ease. And it is enough food to feed a dragon for a week.

Well, to sustain a dragon, at least. I remember fondly some of the feasts of my reign, the hours and hours of eating, the tables piled high. I doubt Leana has ever seen such a feast. All I have to offer her is food little better than peasant fare, and it's food she herself had to carry to me.

My tail flicks with frustration. A dragon has never less deserved such a treasure.

Once all the food is set out, she bows to me again as she passes in front of me, then sets to re-filling the pack with any detritus from what she brought last week.

"May I offer you some food, Leana?"

9

"Thank you, your Majesty," she says, stopping her task to give me another bow. "But I can't take your food."

My tail flicks again. The same as always.

Leana isn't a fool. She knows better than to accept food from a dragon such as me, one who is not worthy of being her mate.

I'm proud of my treasure for knowing her own worth, at least.

"Sit with me at least."

That she does, moving closer to me than I'd expect any human to get. Especially a human who will have been told horror story after horror story about me.

I'm not saying they don't have a basis in truth. I know exactly what I am. But I do think they have had a century to ferment, growing stronger and stronger until the grain of truth might be obscured by the story.

But Leana sinks onto her knees, sitting back on her haunches before me, like she is not afraid of me in the slightest.

I don't know what I did to convince her that I'm safe when any other human would react in fear. I never ask, in case it reminds her to be afraid. I just appreciate what I have.

My legs are chained firmly to the ground, anchors sunk so deep in the stone I couldn't possibly hope to pull them free. My arms are chained too, but I have some movement. I have to, to feed myself. And it would be enough movement to grab up the beautiful young servant kneeling before me.

Not to mention my fire breath, a dragon's greatest and most legendary weapon.

I don't touch her, of course. I will rot in here, never seeing another living being, before I hurt her. I will starve to death here in the darkness before I hurt her. I will cut off my own wings before I hurt her.

According to Leana, my fire breath would not be enough to burn her, not with the fire that lingers underneath her skin. She was chosen to look after me precisely because they were sure I would never be able to burn her. That's an extraordinary amount of fire magic.

Leana is truly a one-of-a-kind treasure. A century ago, her apparent magical abilities would have intrigued me. Now, it's simply every detail about her I find so intriguing.

"Tell me about the world," I request, flicking my claw through the pile of food to select a meal.

"What do you want to know?"

"Whatever you want to tell me. What has happened since you were here last?"

She tells me the basics of her world. I close my eyes and listen to her describe a sunrise, the high water in the river, and the heat of the day. It's almost like I can feel it, just for a moment.

Leana brings me so much more than food. She brings me herself, for the brief moments I can bask in her presence. But she also brings me these small pieces of the outside world, and they're all I have to hold on to when she's gone.

And then our hour is over. Leana gets to her feet with an almost regretful expression on her face and bows deeply once more. "Until next week, your majesty," she says.

"Be well, Leana."

Then my treasure lifts her pack and departs from my prison.

Chapter Three

LEANA

I have to be careful climbing my way out of the prison. No one would come to save me if I fell and broke a leg. Likely no one would even notice for days.

No one but King Osir, who would undoubtedly hear it happen. But what could he do? Chained as he is, all he could do is listen to me. If he were even inclined to help, I remind myself, which he likely wouldn't be.

Just because he's kinder to me than any person in memory doesn't mean he actually cares about me. He's a dragon and a royal to boot, and I'm just a human servant.

His attention sometimes makes me forget that, so I always make sure to remind myself when I leave. I am just the human who brings him food, and he is a lonely prisoner. Of course he pays me special attention; what else does he have to do?

Of course he wants me to enjoy a meal with him, even if he doesn't have the food to spare—who else talks to him civilly? Where else can he get even a moment of normalcy?

Leaving is always the most difficult part. I want to accept the meal, to sit and talk with him. To pretend we'd ever talk to each other outside of the cell.

He listens well, and when he does speak, he's unfailingly polite, far more polite than my station deserves. Something in me aches to stay and continue the conversation every week.

Usually, when I'm climbing out of his prison and away from his piercing eyes, I can remind myself that he killed humans, and he killed his own brothers. That he's a murderer and that he was locked away for a reason. That him being a good conversationalist doesn't forgive him those crimes.

Usually.

At last I can see daylight again. I let the flames on my skin die out, their light no longer needed, and I push open the grate that covers the mouth of the cave.

As I emerge into the day-lit world, I spare a thought for the king who hasn't seen sunlight in a century. What a miserable existence.

Does he deserve it for his crimes? Maybe. I don't know the exact count of people dead because of him, but I know it's too many. But after a century, I do know that if I could give the king anything, I'd want to give him the sky back. Even if

14

it's just a glimpse, just the sight of the sun and the moon above him.

As soon as I'm once again back on solid ground, I drop the pack, giving my shoulders a break from the strain of carrying it.

But it'll have to be a short break. The sun is high in the sky and I have chores to do.

No one planned on me stopping to talk to the king when I brought him his food, and no one has ever allotted me additional time for it. From what the king has told me, I am the first to bother. Several before me merely threw food towards him, and it landed outside of his reach as often as not. That makes my heart rate pick up and my muscles clench in a way I can't quite explain. He's not a difficult man to talk to, even in his towering dragon form. Even with constantly reminding myself of his past, I still find him too easy to talk to. Somehow his words, soothing and deep, always make me forget that. So I let him pull me into conversation every time, and happily too, even if it will make me late returning for my afternoon chores.

I turn to lock the grate behind me, tucking the key back into my tunic before reluctantly lifting the pack again. It would be easier if I could simply dump the garbage here, but I'm told to bring it back. Some poor soul will probably have the task of digging through old chicken bones and often uneaten loaves of moldy bread, like they fear King Osir will somehow smuggle out treasures instead.

With the sun beating down on me and reminding me how much of the day is already gone, I shift the pack on my shoulders and walk back to the castle.

***

Once I arrive, I'm forced to hand off both the pack and the key to a guard on duty. I'm the only one who ever uses the key, but I'm not allowed to keep it. I don't know what they fear I'll do with it. The cave is dangerous and everyone knows what waits for them at the bottom, so I don't expect anyone would want to take the key from me. The key to the grate would hardly help the king chained hand and foot. And if they're worried about me using it when I'm not supposed to—well, they keep me too busy for that.

Once the key is gone, so is any hint of my special position. I'm no longer the servant trusted to look after King Osir—the only one to ever make the journey for more than four weeks, and one of only a few to ever venture into the cave itself. No, without the key, I'm just any other servant.

I fill a bucket and go to scrub floors.

The castle has been active lately, with more dragons than usual in attendance. Usually, the king and the prince, along with their closest advisors, are the only dragons who live here. But in the last few weeks, dozens more have swept down on the palace, always looking like there's some urgent business that they're late for. This has led to many more rooms needing cleaning, and a lot of ducking around corners to stay out of their way.

I've long since learned that it's better for everyone if us humans fade into the background here in the castle. The dragons are happier for it, and we're safer.

I don't know what they're all doing here. That would be something far above the likes of me. But I put every effort into avoiding them.

As I slip completely beneath their notice, I can't help thinking of King Osir. He says my name so gently, in a way I haven't ever heard it before. He tries every visit to share his meager food supply with me, and he asks me to sit and talk to him, which is likely just because he's lonely, but I still feel the weight of all his attention.

King Osir sees me in a way that no one else does, and I have to repeatedly remind myself that I am the only person he sees; of course I would then be interesting to him. It can be hard to remember sometimes.

I don't share this with anyone, of course. Although none of us human servants would have personally been alive to witness King Osir's crimes, the legends have lingered. He's supposed to hate human magic users like me. He's supposed to be coldly, mercilessly violent. There are plenty of people who are still surprised that I come back alive each week.

So I can't talk about it, but it doesn't stop my mind from drifting to his deep, gravelly voice offering me a meal as I scrub floors throughout the afternoon.

***

The days where I visit King Osir always put me behind on my chores. There's usually an unofficial sort of coverage for me, or else I silently shift some chores to the day before or after, and no one of importance notices the difference. But with so much visiting dragon nobility, we're stretched thin and there's simply no way anyone can take a share of my work.

So I finish my tasks well after the usual dinner hour, and, resigned that breakfast will be my only meal of the day, creep up a rickety set of stairs to my room.

The three other girls who share the room are already there. There's not a curfew on castle staff, but I don't know anyone who has the energy to go out at the end of the day. Usually, eating and sleeping take all the energy we have left.

We're lucky, we tell ourselves. We have a place to sleep every night and food in our bellies. Our livelihoods aren't dependent on how good the crops grow every year. And, if we stay out of the way of those above our station, the work isn't really that hard.

Colette, a laundress a few years older than me, holds out a hunk of bread. "All I could spare," she says.

It's more than I ever would have expected, and I take it eagerly, biting into the slightly stale bread with gusto born of significant work done on an empty stomach.

A memory of King Osir once again offering me a meal comes to mind. Like Colette, he has so little to spare.

And like Colette, he offers it for a reason, I remind myself as I take another bite. Colette wants this room to stay peaceful. King Osir wants some company to break up the monotony of his sentence. It doesn't mean anything else.

"You made it back another day, then."

I sit on my pallet, bread still clasped in my hand, and roll my eyes. "It should stop surprising you at some point, Cara." I wiggle to try to get comfortable, despite long ago having learned that there are no remaining comfortable spots.

"You were picked as a sacrifice," Cara says softly. "Sacrifices don't come back, Leana. It'll continue to surprise me."

I don't think that I'm a sacrifice. I don't think Prince Noctere reviewed his staff and decided that I was simply an expendable member of his household. I'd like to think it's because he knows my gifts, and he knew I would be up for this task.

"He won't hurt me. He can't."

She raises an eyebrow. "You put too much faith in your supposed abilities to avoid his fire. He's a dragon, Leana. You have to be smarter; there's plenty of ways they can kill us that your magic won't protect you from."

"I'm well aware." All of us are intimately aware of all the ways dragons could kill us. The recent increase in dragons around the castle has been a stark reminder. But I still say, "I just don't think he's worse than any of the others."

Cara huffs. "He was locked up for killing people like you."

He's never once expressed distaste for what I am, and I've never sought to hide my magic from him. But I don't say that. They've never met him, and I know from experience that I can't convince them, so I let it go.

I finish my bread, then coax the fire a little stronger before lying down to sleep.

***

The next morning, I'm the first one up. As much as I appreciate Colette bringing me a part of her meal, I won't miss another one.

The kitchen is already fairly busy, even with the early hour, so I slip between people, dodging moving plates and platters.

20

Sharp words and pinched brows tell me the extra workload from the dragons visiting the castle is being felt here in the kitchen. I do my best to make myself small and stay out of the way.

"Good morning," I murmur to a woman busy frying bacon while I scoop porridge from the pot meant for castle staff.

She flips the bacon and wipes sweat off her forehead. "Do you know how much bacon I've already fried?"

"Quite a lot, I imagine," I venture.

She sighs and shakes her head. "That lot, always needing more." She looks down at my bowl. "And here we are."

I don't want to discuss this. Here we are. It's true, indisputable and unchangeable. Humans serve dragons. So I just nod and take my bowl and go to eat before starting my chores.

I've only made it through freshening the linens in three rooms before there are frantic footsteps in the corridor. I poke my head out, assuming it must be some noble lord frantically in need of service. But it's Jenessa, a fellow maid, and she's desperately out of breath.

"There you are," she gasps. "I've been sent for you."

I jerk in surprise. "Sent for me?" No one ever sends for me. Not unless my work is in some way unsatisfactory, and I wrack my mind for something I could have failed to do.

Nothing comes to mind, and that somehow makes it worse. If I could pinpoint a specific moment, a task I skipped, a time I was late...

"Who sent for me?"

"Prince Noctere."

It's like the world falls from under my very boots. Prince Noctere wouldn't summon me if a pillow wasn't properly plumped.

It must have to do with the king. The former king, I mean. Prince Noctere directly assigned me the duty, the only time he'd spoken to me in years. It's the only reason I can think of that he'd want to see me. Have I been negligent in my duty in some way?

I could stand here all day, worrying about what I've done, but it won't accomplish anything. So I square my shoulders and nod once, following her out of the room.

I don't know what I expected, truthfully. It was not a courtyard filled with a dozen other mingling servants.

If there's a group of us, a group with servants I don't even recognize, then surely this can't be about something I personally did wrong. Somehow, that doesn't make the trepidation building in my gut any better.

Jenessa fades away before I can ask her if she knows anything, and I can't say I blame her. The tension in the air is palpable, and I wouldn't want to be here if I didn't need to be either.

I reluctantly step into the crowd, waiting for whatever has brought us all here.

I don't have to wait long. Prince Noctere strides into the courtyard, steps powerful and commanding all attention. He's in his human form, but like all dragons, his deep blue scales cover the side of his neck, only partially hidden by a starched collar.

He walks into the courtyard like we've all personally made him late for something important, his brown eyes hard and serious. I'm no expert, but I doubt that's a good sign for any of us.

Usually, I try to avoid dragons looking at me at all. Nothing good ever comes from drawing attention. I do my job and I stay out of the way of the royal family and the nobility, and I find myself safer for it.

Prince Noctere is only a few years older than I am, but everyone knows he's been the unofficial power around here for several years now, and he gets treated like it. Immediate silence descends on the space, and servants begin to bow, nerves making them clumsy.

He surveys the crowd while several advisors stumble to a halt behind him. "All of you are released from your duties," he announces, voice stiff as it carries across the courtyard.

Muffled gasps spread around the crowd. Serving in the castle is a respectable enough job, with decent wages, and a warm place to sleep. Being let go would devastate everyone here.

The thought is almost academic. I can't make it apply to myself. I've never left the castle. I never will, surely. Surely this is not real.

"Please see my staff for your new assignments, effective immediately. All will become clear in time."

No one moves for a long moment, and then the prince actually turns to walk off, leaving us milling about like stunned fish.

An official clears his throat. "Please form orderly lines to receive your new assignments." He might not be the prince, but the level of command in his voice gets us all moving.

I step into a line, nerves churning my stomach. I grip the bottom of my tunic, twisting the fabric. What new assignments? Why now? What will this mean?

Why me?

I thought I was secure. I've been at the castle for my entire life and done everything they've asked of me. I entertained the child prince. I clean. I even take care of the former king. I thought my position was unique, and I never dreamed of anything changing.

A hand clasps on my upper arm. "Not you," a man says. He's dressed like a soldier, but his voice is crisper, cleaner than the average soldier. His hand squeezes, dragging me out of the line. "You have a meeting to attend."

Chapter Four

LEANA

I don't belong in a room like this.

It's a room meant for matters of state. If they handed me a broom and told me to sweep up, I would understand my presence here. But that's not what happens. The soldier escorts me in, grip on my arm not loosening the entire way. Then he pushes me into a chair and takes a position at the door, hands clasped behind his back.

We don't have to wait long. Prince Noctere enters the door at the far end, striding to the chair at the end of the table. "Good. You're here," he says, as if I came willingly. "Leana."

I swallow. "Your highness."

There's protocol to follow. I believe I'm supposed to stand when he enters, although I've already been shoved into a chair, and the soldier looks like he'll happily shove me back into it if I stand. At any rate, Prince Noctere sits and makes no comment on protocol.

Three others follow him in, taking seats around the table. I keep a nervous eye on all of them, all dragons, all members of this court, all far above the likes of me.

Why am I here? What could I possibly have to do with this?

I don't have long to wait. "Every servant we just released is a human magic user," Prince Noctere says. "All magic users have been deemed to be needed elsewhere, outside of simple jobs in the castle."

"Where, your highness?" I dare to ask in desperation for something to start making sense.

Human magic users aren't common in this kingdom anymore, not after so many died a century ago. And most magic users I know have little power. I can't fathom another job that the prince might want them to do.

"We are a kingdom shortly to be at war." He says it staring straight ahead, all inflection removed from his tone, like he's reading the words from some dry report.

The pronouncement sits in the room for a long moment, heavy and suffocating. "War?" I ask.

I would never assume I know or even understand matters of state. But I thought servants overhead everything in this castle, yet this news of war blindsides me.

"The kingdom of Ashar has, it seems, deemed the time ripe for an attack," Prince Noctere continues. "There have been rumblings for a while, of course, but our spies tell us the time is now."

Because of his father. I hear it even if no one speaks it. Because King Braxil hasn't been seen by anyone in over a year.

We are a country with an ailing king and a prince who is young by dragon standards trying to hold it all together. We must look weak and vulnerable for the taking.

"Naturally, everyone with any magic will be immediately assigned duties with the military. They'll be invaluable in upcoming days."

I didn't know every servant in that courtyard, but I know some. And most of them don't have the magic to light a candle, never mind face a dragon at war. I'm getting the picture of why I'm here, though.

Prince Noctere knows perfectly well that I have magic. I can resist the fire of a dragon, and I realize with a sickening lurch that my fire could probably be made into a weapon of its own. I see a vision of me cutting down an entire battalion, roasting them under the fire from my hands, and I want to vomit.

I don't want to become a murderer. I don't want to kill anyone. Fire seems like a terrible way to die.

And then I remember what Cara said last night, the thing that no human who lives near dragons should ever forget. I can survive a dragon's fire, but I can't survive a sword to the gut. I can't survive a dragon's claws or teeth.

It's not like I have a choice, though. The heavy realization of what exactly I'm being told sits like a congealed mass in my gut. "Why was I separated from the others, your highness?" I make myself ask him, trying to keep my voice even as my mind races.

"Everyone else is reporting to military posts tonight. But for you, we have a different assignment. Have you ever heard of the mirror of the oracle?"

"No, your highness." It sounds like a child's bedtime story, and the prince knows full well that neither of us ever heard many bedtime stories.

His lips press together, and he shakes his head. "It's an ancient artifact of some power. Last seen in the possession of my uncle."

King Osir. I grip my tunic, twisting the fabric, starting to see the pieces of his plan coming together.

"What does the mirror do, your highness?" I dare ask.

He waves it away, but won't meet my eyes. "It hardly matters. The point is, he had it last. It's a part of why he was imprisoned, truthfully, although we don't have time for that sordid tale, and I imagine it would just bore you."

I hold very still. We both know it would not bore me. We both know he's keeping a secret from me.

But what else can I do but allow it? We both know our roles with each other, after all. It's always been the same.

"The point is, an item like the mirror could turn the tides in this war. The princes of Ashar might also be after it, given what it does. I doubt you're well appraised of international politics, but Ashar is experiencing a bit of a succession crisis. The new king is fighting with his brothers over who is to claim their throne, and—" One of the advisors cuts him off by clearing his throat. "Yes, right. Anyways, I want it first."

"Do you not have it, your highness?"

"My uncle hid it from all and refused to turn over its location, even under the threat of torture. And that is where you come in."

"Me? I am not a torturer," I say. I try to sound like I'm not arguing—nothing good ever comes out of arguing—but I can't let him think I have it in me to go and torture the king.

"Of that I'm well aware. I have torturers, Leana. No, you are something else. He's fond of you, or as fond as he is of anyone, I've heard. He must be, to let you come in and out unharmed for so long."

"He has no one else," I protest, forgetting myself momentarily.

He smiles, clearly proud of himself, and his eyes tighten with a sort of cruelty it hurts to see on him. "Exactly. So he will answer your questions."

I doubt that. King Osir is unfailingly polite, but we are not friends. He is not going to divulge secrets to me.

I think unwillingly of the day he tried to tell me where I could find a host of jewels he had hidden, because they are not the same situation. He'd simply been offended by my plainness, which I can't blame a dragon for.

"What am I to do for you, your highness?" I ask, preferring to get to the point.

"There is still a cabin near the prison, right? We had guards stationed there, when he was first imprisoned. You can stay there. Someone will bring supplies out to you. Spend every moment with him, if that's what it takes. I don't care if you move into that damned prison. Get him to tell you where he hid the cursed mirror, and report back here only when you know."

"I—yes, okay, I—alright," I stumble through my words, not knowing what to say. "Your highness," I add on belatedly, mind still lost, thoughts racing ahead to the task I've been assigned.

"Good." Prince Noctere stands, and this time I remember protocol enough to do the same. He nods at the soldier still by the door. "And Leana?"

I swallow. "Yes, your highness?"

"Understand me very carefully. You've been helpful to us these past few years, and you might be helpful again. But I know your gifts better than anyone, and if you can't do this job, if you take too long—I would rather have you on the front line than in that prison. Every pawn serves its purpose, one way or another. So, either get results, or be prepared to fight. Do you understand?"

I understand. I remember when his tutor taught him to play chess like it was yesterday, and I remember him sharing his father's strict lessons around the game. I know exactly what he means. Get the supposed mad king to tell me a secret he was imprisoned for a century ago, or be sent to die in war.

Chapter Five

OSIR

The creak of that old, rusted grate opening wakes me from a dead sleep.

I cock my head, listening. I know it is difficult to track time down here, but I have not eaten enough of the food for it to be time for my treasure to return to me. But I would recognize those footfalls anywhere. It's her. Leana.

When at last she emerges into my cavern, hands glowing with flames, I look her over frantically. Perhaps she's hurt. Perhaps something has happened. But if that was true, then I am worse than useless to her, all the way down here.

I can't smell any blood, nor see any wounds. She walks with even strides, without a limp or any apparent pain.

She doesn't have the heavy pack, I realize belatedly. Something is different about this visit after all.

"I realize my grasp on time is poor," I say, my voice deep and raspy from not speaking since she last left. "But I don't think it has been nearly long enough since you've been here last."

She bows, deeply and sincerely, as she always does despite its ridiculousness. Who bows to a prisoner in chains? "I apologize for disturbing you, your majesty."

I rumble my discontent. "You never apologize to me, Leana. Least of all for that. You could not disturb me." There had been a time, I faintly remember, where that was not true. Where I had pursued knowledge across the entire known world and beyond, and had my books and tomes and artifacts, and would have considered any interruption the greatest affront, even for matters of state.

Maybe it's the time and the boredom, but I like to think a large part of it is simply her, my beautiful treasure.

"How long has it been, Leana?" I probe, eyeing her carefully, like she will provide some sort of clue as to why she's here.

"A day."

My tail flicks. "A day? You've never been back so quickly." She has not stepped closer to me, nor lit the torches in my cell. Instead, she stands stiffly by the mouth of the cavern, still illuminated only by her own flickering flames. She hasn't been so rigid and unsure around me in years. "Come, sit. Explain to me what's happened."

She nods, lighting the torches as she comes closer, then sinks into her usual position in front of me, kneeling and then sitting back on her heels. "I'm worried you'll be angry when I tell you," she admits, voice soft.

"I could never be angry at you," I tell her immediately, and it's true. Leana can do no wrong. She could admit to me she has come back today as my new torturer and I don't think I could muster even an ounce of anger. I would just be grateful for the time with her.

The idea is ridiculous, of course. My Leana is too gentle to be a torturer.

"Tell me," I prompt, trying to keep my voice soft. It's a difficult thing to do in this form, considering how my voice is naturally loud, rumbling up from my chest. But even so, I must succeed, because she nods, seemingly bolstered. Her shoulders slide back, and she lifts her head to look me in the eye.

"Have you heard of the mirror of the oracle?" she asks, and I almost think I heard wrong.

"Did my brother put you up to this?" I ask. That mirror should have been confined to the past. Certainly not something the very young, currently mortal woman in front of me knows about.

"Your nephew, actually, your majesty."

I didn't even know I had a nephew. I'm sure he's just as obnoxious as his father. He must be, if he's sending Leana here to ask me stupid questions.

Stupid question or not, she is here just a day after she last left, and I'm selfishly glad to see her. My nephew has done me a favor, really. "What does he want to know about it?"

"He wants to know where it is, your majesty."

"No."

Her shoulders slump, and I already regret my words, ache to take them back to take that look from her. But she speaks before I can formulate what to say. "Of course, your majesty. I understand. Only..." She hesitates here, biting her lip and turning her head.

"Only what, Leana?" I prod. My scales itch with how wrong this is, with how much I despise her looking so unsure.

"No, your majesty. Please forget it. It was a selfish concern."

Selfish? This treasure who has climbed down here, risking serious injury, week after week for years, just to make sure I don't starve? This treasure who has spoken to me with more kindness than I have ever deserved? Selfish?

"Be selfish, Leana," I command.

It takes a long moment for her to speak. "There's a war coming," she admits, voice so soft that I'd miss it if there was a single other sound in this cavern. "And I was told I'd be sent to the front lines if I cannot retrieve the mirror."

A deep, primal rage rushes through my body, turning my mind off and causing me to shake. Leana. My treasure. My treasure, my mate, given such an ugly ultimatum. Sent to war.

Leana doesn't move, but a look of fear crosses her face, and it's only then that I realize that this internal anger has been made external, that my rumbling has been enough to shake the cavern.

I force myself to calm down, although I can't quite quench the raging inferno of anger inside me. Still, I must look calm. I won't scare her. "Tell me," I grit out. "Tell me exactly what happened."

So she does, recounting the events of the day in a flat, too-even voice. It sounds like she's telling me a story that happened to someone else, and she does a remarkable job keeping her distance from it. If not for the slight tremor in her hand where it rests on her thigh, I'd never know the difference.

There are large pieces of her story missing. Information she was not given, history she would have no hope of knowing.

Some of those pieces I can fill in myself. She does not know the significance of the mirror or the reason a war might be fought over it. But I do.

I found the mirror a little over a century ago, rescued it from legend, and brought it back to our kingdom. I'd read about it for decades before I found it. I knew its legends. I knew the power it could bestow, and I selfishly took full advantage. And then I hid it and killed for it, and was imprisoned over it. I've even been tortured over it.

I consider my treasure before me, still kneeling, waiting for me to speak, to respond to the story she just told me. What would she see if she looked in that damn mirror?

No doubt something far better than I did. She would wield the knowledge far better, too.

What does a servant girl, a mortal-for-now, see when shown how to achieve true power?

The version of me who existed a century ago would have scoffed at the idea. The me in this cell, who sees the quiet strength and determination in her face, wants intensely to know.

If I could bring her to where I hid it, I would show it to her in a heartbeat. I would tell no one of its location but her.

But it doesn't matter, because I wouldn't be telling her. I would be telling my nephew, who no doubt works on his father's behalf and is the type who threatens young servants with the front lines of a war.

My tail flicks as I think. I cannot tell her. I cannot send her away empty-handed. I cannot, cannot let her go to war, where she'll no doubt be cut down and I will lose my treasure.

The thought of her going to war is like a spike through my heart. I was once a great dragon, and I once could have protected her as she deserves. Now I am practically nothing.

Chained here beneath the earth, not knowing what has happened to her until she dies and both our lives end.

"Can I convince you to run away?" I ask her. "I still have wealth, Leana. I can tell you where to find enough to start a life as a fine lady somewhere."

She's already shaking her head. Why couldn't she just be selfish? "I have nowhere to go," she admits softly.

I want to argue that riches can open many doors, but perhaps she's right. If war really is coming, any safety would only be temporary.

When dragons go to war, humans pay the price. I learned that the hard way, and I haven't let myself forget it.

I flick my tail again, bashing it against the rock wall a few times. I hardly notice. "The reality is I cannot give you what you seek," I say slowly, weighing my options. "That mirror won't end a war. It will just make it worse."

"Oh." Her voice is so quiet I can barely hear it.

I consider for a moment. My bastard nephew told her to spend every day with me if she needs to, to get the answer.

She can spend every day with me. Every day she is here is a day she is not being sent to war, and it's another day for me to think.

"Give me time, Leana," I implore. "Let me think."

She should argue, perhaps. But she doesn't. "Of course, your majesty."

***

"They gave you a cabin to live in?" I verify some hours later, after asking her for every detail of her story twice more, probing for anything else she might have heard or known.

Her mouth quirks into a smile that looks more bitter than I would expect from her. "Prince Noctere remembered it was there. He said there used to be guards stationed there." Guards, perhaps. Torturers, more likely. The quest for the mirror is not a new one. "I've gone in there before. It's not in a great state to live in."

"Stay with me," I say immediately, as if what I have to offer her is any improvement. I am trapped in a cavern deep underground, left in nearly perpetual darkness, with no way to tell day and night and no company. It's enough to drive someone mad.

At least I have food, though, and a roof over my head not in danger of caving in or exposing her to the elements and wild animals.

What a pitiful dragon I've become, to be proud of the bare minimum.

If my plans do not somehow end with this treasure being given the finest bed in a castle and food until she cannot possibly eat any more, then the plan should be discarded entirely as worthless.

She tilts her head, then smiles again, this time with less bitterness. Unless I miss my mark, I think that might actually be a touch of deviousness in her smile. "I suppose the chances of someone coming down here to drag me off to war are low," she muses.

If only it were that easy. But it is as good a temporary measure as any, so I nod. "Exactly. I assure you, very few want to come down here. And if my insipid nephew makes the journey himself..." I let the thought hang, because truthfully, I don't want to explain to her that I'd like the chance to give him a thrashing. Not that I can do much, chained as I am.

I haven't eaten anything since before I fell asleep, and I can feel the hunger. "Can I offer you some food, Leana?" I ask hesitantly.

"Thank you, your majesty," she says. "I'd be honored to share your food."

And then she reaches into my pile of food and pulls out some bread and cheese, which they always include when they send her with food, despite the fact that only meat will ever satisfy me in this form. I watch as she takes a bite of the bread with bated breath.

Sharing food is not an official mark of anything, but it is certainly an indication of intention. Dragons share so little. Surely this means something to her.

"Aren't you going to eat, your majesty?" she asks, self-consciously lowering her meal after only the one bite.

"I'm savoring," I tell her.

"Savoring what? You haven't eaten anything to savor yet."

"You've never agreed to eat my food before," I say.

"I have never stayed here before," she points out.

"If you stay with me, I will protect you," I vow, taking the liberty to edge my large head closer to her. "I have accepted your food several hundred times now, Leana, and I am honored you would accept mine today."

She doesn't flinch away from me, so I dare move slightly closer. Her whole body is the size of my head, but somehow, I don't think I scare her.

"Thank you for sharing with me," she says simply, clutching her bread.

"Don't thank me, Leana. Everything I have is yours. I'm aware it's currently not much, but I will swear it all to you anyways. And I will do whatever necessary to someday be able to provide what you deserve."

Leana is silent for a long moment. Thinking over my offer, I assume. The next step would be to present her jewelry, the finest I could find, a piece that truly speaks to who she is. But I have nothing to give to her, and it's probably too soon. She's too young. Too mortal. She isn't ready yet.

I am not ready yet, I remind myself furiously, looking around the cavern I'm trapped in. I add another step to my plan: I will not ask anything else of her until I'm in the position to offer her everything she deserves.

While I've been refining my plan, Leana seems to have done some thinking of her own. She looks at me with a furrowed brow, and asks, "Your majesty, worthy of what, exactly?"

Chapter Six

LEANA

The cavern is as still as death for a long moment.

"You are my mate, my most beloved treasure," he says, voice a rumble that shakes loose stones. It makes the pronouncement sound resonant and kingly, even if it's just made to little old me.

It's the words that confuse me as much as the tone. Mate?

His tail flicks again, as it does whenever he gets frustrated. "You didn't know."

"I—no, your majesty," I stammer. I at least have the presence of mind to still make an appropriate response when royalty addresses me.

The king is already lying directly on the ground, to bring him closer to my level. Even with this relaxed posture, I swear he droops somehow. "I thought you declined my offers of food, knowing they weren't worthy of you. Knowing they could never be worthy of you."

I squeak. "I didn't accept your food because I never brought you enough, and I couldn't stand to take food you needed."

Something around his eyes, usually so sharp and vigilant, goes soft in a way I've never seen before. "Kind mate," he rasps. "Far kinder than I'd ever deserve. Everything I have is equally yours, treasure."

Treasure? And while I know he is a prisoner, and he has nothing, King Osir is a king. He still talks about his former hoards of precious items. What is he doing, offering half of it to a mere servant so easily?

My frantic thoughts are broken by his snout bumping my leg. The move is gentle, barely a nudge, but even that light contact makes everything inside me slow. "Eat your meal, treasure," the king commands gently. "You must eat. You need your strength."

I take a bite before I even think through what is being asked. It's instinctual, of course, to listen to orders. I've been taking them my whole life.

His large black eyes watch me, waiting for a reaction.

I take another bite, and he rumbles, the movement making his rough scales scrape lightly on my clothes.

"You should eat too," I manage to say.

He moves faster than I can blink, taking one of the many cuts of meat I bring over every week and swallowing it seemingly whole. "Thank you for the meal, treasure," he says, already returning to my side. He doesn't touch me, but I can feel the heat radiating off his scales through my clothes.

I've never seen any of the dragons around the castle like this, unguarded and affectionate. I suppose I only see them rarely, in more official moments. And I never see them in private moments with their mates.

The last mated dragon I saw was Prince Noctere's mother and father, I think. But I don't ever remember seeing King Braxil and his human mate in the same room together. It was no secret how much they hated each other.

I somehow doubt King Braxil called her treasure and watched her eat with eager eyes.

I have no knowledge to bring into this strange situation. I'm at a distinct disadvantage here, and I find myself needing to catch up.

"Please tell me more about what it means to be your mate," I ask, the words still sounding ridiculous as they come out of my mouth.

He rumbles again. Like a cat purring, I think, although I would never dare compare the dragon in front of me to a house cat. "What do you wish to know?"

"Everything, your majesty. Whatever you're willing to tell me."

"First off, I am not your king, treasure."

I consider how to approach that for a moment. Technically speaking, King Osir is no one's king. Not anymore. Not in my lifetime. But to say so sounds downright disrespectful. The man was a king. He lives in chains. I will not take his title from him too.

"You're still a king," I say.

"I'm glad you think so," he says amicably. "I like to think I am, and that someday, I will have the chance to prove it again. But even so, I am not your king. You have no king."

"Of course I do. Your majesty," I remember to add belatedly.

His lip curls, and dragons cannot smirk, but I think he means to. "To call me your king would imply that I rule you, and I do not rule my mate. To call anyone else your king implies they rule us both, and I simply cannot give my brother that satisfaction."

I could never even begin to comprehend how to respond to that.

Yesterday, I was sweeping floors and making beds. I had no need to navigate this type of interaction.

"What do I call you, then?" I ask him.

He rumbles against me again. "That rather depends on you, treasure. Anything you call me will be lovely. We can start with my name."

"Osir," I breathe. It feels wrong to say it. It feels like I should be punished for saying it, and I almost brace for a strike before I realize there isn't one coming.

"My name on your lips is a blessing, treasure. Now that we have established what you will call your mate, what else do you wish to know?"

"Everything," I tell him. "I don't know anything. I knew King—your brother," I hastily correct, not wanting to discuss names yet again, "I know of your brother and his human mate, but that's all."

He perks up at that, moving so he's sitting more upright. "Braxil mated?"

"Queen Cassandra. She was a foreign princess. I'm only here because of her—my mother was her servant, brought from her own homelands. She and your brother had a son."

"But are they mated?" he asks, tail flicking.

I shrug. "I think so, but I don't know anything. Those aren't the type of things people like me are told."

"How did they meet?"

"If I remember correctly, he visited her court and proposed on the spot." At least, that's the story my mother told me when I'd asked.

"Mates, then. But you said was. She can't be dead." He says it with great assurance, fully confident in his conclusion.

I don't have the heart to remind him how easily humans die.

"We haven't seen her in years. She left without telling anyone well over a decade ago. She left in the middle of the night, taking only my mother with her. We don't know where she is."

"Interesting."

"What's interesting?" I dare to ask.

"She rejected the mating bond. That's unfortunate. If I wasn't here, I might feel bad for my brother."

And we are back to yet another thing I simply don't understand. "What does that mean?"

"Dragons mate for life, but mates can reject the bond, even if they accepted it initially. It's always their right to change their mind."

"Accept the bond," I repeat, stuck on that. "Is that what I did when I took your food?"

He lies back down, once more putting his head right next to me. "You made me the happiest dragon in existence, but the food is just a promise. It's not binding, nor will I hold you to it if you realize you are worth far more than this."

"I need to know how the bond works," I insist. "I don't understand it at all."

"Dragons are greedy and selfish creatures, and we know when a perfect treasure falls into our laps," he says, and I don't miss how soft his eyes are when he says perfect treasure. "And when the treasure is living and breathing and not, say, a fine necklace, we will do whatever it takes to keep it."

"You'll feed them," I say doubtfully.

"A dragon worthy of their treasure will start by providing for them," he corrects. "Showing that they can provide, and provide well. That they are worthy of such a treasure and that they can provide adequate care. As you can see, I have been sorely lacking on that front, and believe me, treasure, it's not escaped my notice and I'm most embarrassed."

I almost tell him about the stale bread I ate for dinner last night, but decide that he might react poorly to that, so I keep my mouth shut.

Some part of me wants to ask how he would prove he could provide for me, if he were free. But it's a foolish thought and I squash it down. King Osir isn't free. He hasn't been free in a century and likely never will be again. "So that's it?"

"No. The food is simply the first act. A dragon will prove to their mate, over and over, that they can provide. And eventually, if they accept, there will be a mark. An agreement."

"What sort of mark?"

"I would have you in the finest jewels, my treasure. A thousand gems, just for you. All of them the most beautiful pieces in my hoard, to be worthy of you. But there would be one piece, the first piece. If you took it, you'd accept the bond. And I would be honored beyond measure."

I think of Queen Cassandra. I have no memory of her wearing any jewels at all.

"And it works the same, even though I'm human?" I ask.

49

"Human or dragon, I know the best when I see it. And, Leana, you are the best. The finest treasure in the world. Make no mistake."

Something inside me has gone soft and warm, getting softer every single time he compliments me again. I try to sternly warn myself off. Surely this is just the product of too long alone.

Kings don't think of servants as fine treasures. They just don't. And I'll have to keep reminding myself of that, or else I fear this warm feeling will take over entirely.

Chapter Seven

OSIR

My treasure is having trouble accepting what I'm explaining to her. That's fine. She's human, and I can't expect her to instantly understand the mind of a dragon.

I will gladly tell her her worth every day, every hour, for the rest of my existence if that's what she needs.

I could list out a thousand ways she's wonderful and give her one every hour. Then, when I'm done, I'll have a thousand more ready for her.

Of course, that's partially because I am only good for words right now. Pretty words, perhaps, but still intangible words. Everything a dragon should provide to prove their worth to a mate remains sadly out of my reach.

I look at the chains wrapped around my front limbs, considering them. I'd grown accustomed to my situation long before Leana stumbled into my life. But now I must plan a way out of it.

I cannot simply hand over the cursed mirror. It would solve the immediate problem of her being sent to war, but it would cause its own host of problems. Chiefly, that no one should ever have that mirror.

I flex one giant clawed foot in my chains. I've tugged at them for decades, systematically trying to weaken them. They never budge.

If I was free, I'd give Leana the world.

"You have more questions?" I ask my treasure, turning my attention back to her.

"A thousand, I think," she admits. "But even I don't know them all."

"What's on your mind?" I ask, eager to know any of the thoughts so often hidden behind her soft eyes.

"I don't understand what being a mate means," she blurts out, the words spilling from her like a dam has failed. "You keep talking about what you'd do for me, what you'd give to me, but I don't understand what I'm meant to do for you."

I hold very still. My first instinct is to tell my mate that nothing in her life should be about what she can give to others. That she is a treasure who should demand things for herself. But of course her life has not ever given her proof of that.

"My understanding is that there is some similarity to human spouses," I say after a moment. "What would you do with a spouse?" I regret it the moment the words escape me. I don't want to hear about her and some fictional other person.

What if they're not fictional? What if my treasure has considered, maybe even desires, some human?

Then I must step up my plans so I can prove to her that I am simply more worthy of her than this theoretical human. I sit up and turn to take more food so she can't see this thought on my face. I don't wish to scare her, or have her think my rage at some perhaps non-existent human could ever be for her.

"I have no concept of what to do with a spouse," she says, voice sounding half strangled. "I've never considered it. The only thing I know about it is children." Her words trail off, but I realize she is looking low on my body, between my legs.

It takes me a long moment and some peering at her delightfully flushed face to realize what she means.

Yes, human spouses and dragon's mates both fuck, although this form is not for that. This body only has its uses in protecting her and providing for her. It can hunt and kill and shelter her. For the finer points of providing for her needs, I'd need to be able to take my human form again.

To put it bluntly, a dragon's shaft is as big as her entire body, while my human form's cock, while still quite large, is a much more manageable size for my human treasure.

I mentally amend my plan. Escape from this place. Destroy the threat that is my nephew and perhaps the entire damn nation of Ashar if need be. Lavish my mate with every finery in the world. And then pleasure her until all she can do is moan my name.

"Do you want children, Leana?" I ask.

"I never... I haven't..." she continues to stutter, looking anywhere but at me. "I never considered it," she finally says, pulling herself together. "I've done everything in my power to avoid it."

I study her face, flushed and perhaps a little intimidated. "I promise you, my human form could make you feel things you never even imagined."

She won't look directly at me. "I don't doubt it. I never imagined..."

Is my mate a virgin? The thought sends a shiver through my scales. I'd never be upset if she wasn't, but as a dragon, I can't help but see it as one more treasure for me to hoard.

I don't ask, though. There's a difference between making her flush and making her truly uncomfortable, and anyway, I fear I haven't properly answered her question yet.

"As your mate, I would pleasure you however you desire," I tell her. "And provide for every need, and your comfort. Children or no children. Whatever you want."

A thousand images race through my mind, all of them of her warm, pink cunt, her hard nipples, her flushed face and slack, well-fucked expression. What I wouldn't give to know what they look like for real, instead of relying on my imagination.

I've always had a powerful imagination, though.

"You're still saying things you'll do for me. Not what you expect of me," she reminds me, forcing my thoughts back to the present.

I think too much has been expected of my treasure. That too many people have put demands on my Leana. And that I have no qualms about using my fire on anyone else who might try.

"I expect you to enjoy your life. Revel in it. And spend it by my side," I say carefully. "Does that seem like something you can do?"

Her breath catches, but slowly, she nods.

She doesn't argue. She so rarely argues, but this time I think it might be genuine exhaustion and not just timidness preventing her.

I lie down again, but this time, I don't try to keep my distance. I wrap around her until I have her pressed where my neck meets my skull, her warmth making the scales there tingle. "We'll talk more tomorrow," I tell her. Or whatever passes for tomorrow down here, at any rate. "You must be exhausted. Sleep."

She runs a hesitant hand along my neck, and I rumble in satisfaction. Leana has never touched me before. "You're so warm."

I'm full of fire, burning hot and bright. Just looking for an outlet.

"I'm sorry I don't have a proper bed to offer you."

She actually leans fully into my side, her head resting on my scales. "It's okay," she murmurs. "I've slept in far worse places. You're actually quite comfortable."

I owe my mate the softest mattress in the castle, but the feeling of her sleeping against me, trusting me like this? It will never be replicated, not with all the gold in the kingdom.

Chapter Eight

LEANA

I wake up slowly, entirely warm and content. I have no memory of ever feeling like this, this slow and lazy, in my life. Honestly, if it weren't for the scratching sensation under my cheek, I might have even slept longer.

I open my eyes to the dim light of the cave, and the first thing I see is rough scales. Yesterday comes back to me.

The mirror, and Prince Noctere's ultimatum. King Osir, who insists I do not call him king, who must really be mad to think a servant is his mate.

Has a mad man ever had sweeter words?

Maybe I'm just a fool. Maybe that's all it is, that every one of his words makes me feel soft and longing.

Some girls around the castle have spoken about men with smooth words, the type who know exactly what to say to lure you into bed and then leave you after. I'm sure with his years of experience, the king could be like that.

I don't want to believe it. I want to listen to his gentle words. I want to believe them. But that would make me as mad as he is.

He knows I'm awake. "Good morning, treasure," he says. His voice makes the portion of his neck that I've been using as a pillow shake.

"Good morning, your—"

"What did we say about titles, Leana?" he interrupts to ask.

I hesitate. Titles are a fact of life, but so is giving into the whims of royalty. "Good morning, Osir," I correct. The name feels funny in my mouth, but it's slightly easier to say today than it was yesterday.

"Or whatever passes as morning, in this hellhole, at any rate," he mumbles. I look around and take his point.

"The torches will be burned out soon," I notice. They've never been lit this long before, and we can usually make a torch last for months worth of visits. But neither of us extinguished them yesterday.

His tail flicks. "When they burn out, you must leave me here. I won't have my treasure live in darkness."

"Don't be silly," I say, holding up a burning hand. "I could never be left in darkness."

I can't leave him. I have nowhere to go without that mirror. And King Osir was right when he said anyone would think twice about coming to drag me away from him to send me to war. No one but me ever wants to venture down here.

The king is watching the flames dance across my hand. "You're powerful," he says, approval clear in his voice. "Very powerful."

I extinguish the flames. "Nothing compared to what a dragon can do."

"You're not a dragon. You don't literally have a belly full of fire. All that flame, in such a little package," he argues, eyeing me with what I think might be appreciation.

"And they'll send me to war for it." I can't stop myself from saying it.

It's not that I thought I was owed anything special. I just assumed that if I did my job, kept my head down, and didn't make any trouble, then I'd be taken care of in turn. I should have known better. How many times have I reminded myself that humans are expendable around the castle? And here I am, disappointed because I was reminded of exactly that.

His whole expression darkens. "I will do everything in my power to prevent that."

He won't be able to prevent it. He might be a temporary deterrent, but he won't stop them forever. Not unless he gives over the mirror, and I know he won't.

"Did you sleep well, treasure?" he asks, abruptly changing the subject and shifting my thoughts.

"Very well." It's the truth, too. He's warm and, despite his scales being scratchy, he was relatively comfortable underneath me all night.

His tail flicks. "You deserve a better bed than a cave floor."

"I didn't sleep on the cave floor. I slept on you."

"That is the only redeeming quality of last night," he pronounces. "And I fear it's a selfish one, because as comfortable as I was with my treasure in my possession all night, I can't imagine it was very comfortable for you. You should be asleep on the softest mattress this entire kingdom has available."

I snort. "I sleep on a pallet that lost its shape years ago, directly on the floor in a room with three other girls. The other girls consider themselves lucky to sleep there because as long as we can find wood, at least we know I can light the fire and the room won't be cold," I tell him.

He actually growls at that, the sound deep and rumbling. The hairs on my arm stand on end.

"That should never happen," he insists, and I relax. He's not angry with me.

"Servants are treated that way," I tell him. Humans are treated that way, I don't say.

How many humans did the mad king kill? I doubt I'll find much sympathy there.

"My mate will not be treated in such a way," he insists firmly, leaving no room for argument. "The finest bed in the castle. The biggest, too."

"Why would it need to be big?"

"Because I fully intend to be in that bed every night you'd have me."

I look him over, dozens of times larger than me. "I don't think you'd fit in even the biggest bed I've ever seen."

He actually chuckles at that. I think it's a chuckle, at least; the deep, rasping noise sounds more like a rockslide than any laughter. "My human form, treasure."

"Then why would it need to be so big?" I try to picture his human form. I can't quite make the red scales fade from my view. I'm sure he would be large; I can't imagine a dragon being small. Would he be handsome? Would he look like his brother, pinch-faced and pale?

I've heard the other humans around the castle talking about the people they find attractive, the ones they want to spend time with. I've firmly ignored those conversations for years. But now all I can do is think about what his human form might look like. Would he be beautiful?

"I'm sure they do, treasure, but you've never known the passion of a dragon. We'll need space. You'll thank me for it later."

I flush when I catch his meaning. "We'll—oh."

Intimacy. He's talking about intimacy. I've heard enough whispers, overheard too many comments to not understand. I just never imagined it applying to me.

I've known better than to get involved with anyone. Too many girls have been left behind, hurt, unwanted after one night. My own existence is proof enough of that.

And here is a king, telling me we'll need a big bed so he can properly make love to me.

Why? Is it because I'm the only person he's seen in years? Surely, if he really believes he'll be free of this prison someday, he'll find someone more appropriate to his station.

I remind myself of this, because his sweet words and piercing eyes are starting to make me forget. For a brief moment, I entertain the thought of him holding me in some over-large bed.

I clear my throat, trying to get some semblance of control back. "You're very confident that we'll have this future," I say. A diplomatic way to say you're very confident you'll get free.

"I would never dare be anything else," he says. "Not with your future on the line. Make no mistake, Leana; I have not lied to you. I will make a plan to free us. And I will give you the life you've always deserved."

Deserved. What a ridiculous word. What do I deserve?

"You need to eat," he says when I can't muster a response. "I can provide that much, at least, even if the bed has to wait."

I shake my head. "If I keep eating regular meals, your food will run out far too soon. I hope they send someone to resupply you in a week, but I'm not sure—"

"If the food runs out, then I will simply not eat," he interrupts. "My body is large and takes quite a lot of energy when I need to really use it. As you can see, I barely move down here, so even a little bit of food can last me longer. But even so, I will go hungry before you miss a single meal, treasure."

The words pierce through the mental defenses I just built like a knife through butter. He doesn't need to say anything like this. There is no benefit for him, nothing he can win by saying such sweet words.

I can't decide if that makes the words more or less likely to be sincere.

I bite my lip. I've never argued with royalty before. But I've also never been presented with such a ridiculous order, either.

Besides, the prince once told me it was my task to care for his uncle and keep him alive. So, in a way, when I cross my arms and plant my feet, I still am following orders. "If you don't eat, I won't eat. I'll not have you hungry, and you need more food than I do."

"Stubborn human," he says, and it sounds almost approving. "We'll both eat. And we'll hope my insufferable family remembers that there are two of us here now, and deems it worth their time to feed us."

He sits up, and it's only then that I realize how comforting his warmth has been. I'm not used to feeling cold, given my own fire, but when he leaves, it's like a blanket has been ripped away.

He does return quickly enough, although he doesn't wrap himself around me again, and I don't ask. Instead, he presents me with a meal, bread and the drumstick of a chicken.

"Thank you," I say as I take it, once again touched by his insistence on taking care of me.

He's mad, I remind myself again. Mad and lonely. Surely that explains it.

"I have thought of a plan," he pronounces when I am part way through eating. "Or the beginnings of one."

"Oh?" I ask, pausing to give him my full attention. "What's your plan?"

"How long is the journey back to the castle from here?"

"Just over an hour. Why?"

"So close?" he asks, almost to himself. I want to argue that it's not close at all, not when I have a pack filled with food to contend with, but I take his meaning. He could fly there in minutes if he was free. "I'm going to send you back."

"I don't want to go," I protest before I can think better of arguing with a king. "Please don't send me."

64

His chains rattle, and then he growls. I flinch—I shouldn't have argued with a king—but then I see him huff and lower himself so he's pressed against me once more.

Was he trying to reach for me? To comfort me?

My heart softens a bit. I don't want a dragon reaching for me. There are many reasons why not, not the least being the lethal claws. But the gesture is a kindness I didn't expect.

Between the food, and the words, and the desire to comfort, I have to remind myself yet again that trusting a dragon, and a royal one at that, is a poor plan.

"I will never send you away, treasure," he promises. "Especially not when going back is dangerous. But I don't have a full plan to save you from this asinine war yet. So here are my thoughts: I am sending you back to my nephew with demands."

"Demands?" I barely squeak out, and he rubs his large head against my side.

"My demands. Let him believe you're making progress. That I said I'd give you the mirror in exchange for small comforts here. I will not have my mate live in the darkness, even if you have fire in your blood. And I won't have you go hungry, or sleep on the ground." He rubs his head along me again, and I relax into the touch, feeling the comfort intended by the gesture. "I don't have a full plan yet, treasure. I will think of one. In the meantime, this will provide you some small comforts, and lead him to think you're making progress, buying us time."

I think it over. He has a point—Prince Noctere is less likely to send soldiers here to demand I go to join the military if he thinks I'm making progress towards his goal. "What's on your list, then?"

CHAPTER NINE

LEANA

I have to reject several of the items on his list. I can't ask the prince to provide silk bed sheets or a mattress. He'd know immediately that they aren't for the king, because a fully turned dragon has no use for such things. And there would be no way to explain why the king wishes for me to have such ridiculous luxuries.

Arguing with King Osir feels like fighting against a mountain, or perhaps a storm; I am too small in front of him, my voice matters too little in the discussion, and I would never attempt such a thing. But I can't ask Prince Noctere for a bed, or silk, or the diamond bracelets he requests later.

So I summon up my voice to protest. "Your Majesty, I can't..." I say tremulously, voice weak and faltering.

But he doesn't shout over me, or command. I find him listening, and while he argues back, he doesn't stop me from responding. And, at last, he gives in.

To tell the truth, I think he asks for the diamond bracelets just to make me argue with him again.

What kind of king wants servants to argue with him? A lonely one, maybe.

When at last I have a working list, one we both can tolerate, I prepare to leave to go back to the castle, already thinking over what I'll say to the prince.

"Come back to me soon," the king commands in his deep, rumbly voice.

"I will," I promise, wishing I could touch him, reassure us both. Which is a foolish idea, of course. He knows I'll be back because he's my safety right now, and because he's a king and he's commanded it.

And I shouldn't want to touch him, of course. I can't forget that.

"Be safe," he adds.

"I always am." And with one more long look at him, I begin the journey from his prison.

***

The walk is long and hot, but it's far easier without a pack on my back.

When I make it to the castle, I'm shown inside rather quickly.

"Leana," Prince Noctere says, sweeping into the room I've been led to. "You're back quickly. Was my uncle so easy to break?"

I raise an eyebrow at his wording. "You said I wasn't a torturer, your highness."

He waves a hand as he sits. "You know what I mean. So—where is it?"

I bite my lip; King Osir spoke with such confidence when outlining his plan, and now I need to have my own confidence.

But the reality is, making demands of royalty isn't something I do. I would never dream of it before yesterday.

"The former king has sent me with a list of demands," I tell him, doing my best to keep my voice soft and non-threatening, but also firm, so he knows my visit is sincere. I square my shoulders but can't make myself look him fully in the eyes. "He wants better living conditions in exchange for the mirror."

He huffs, leaning back in the chair to the point of almost reclining. It's very unprincely behavior, and I can almost hear his childhood nanny scolding him for it. I keep the thought firmly to myself.

69

"He should consider himself grateful that he has living conditions at all," he grumbles.

"Nevertheless," I say, making myself be brave enough to press forward, "I don't know how to get the location of the mirror from him without this."

He stares at me for a long moment, then seems to deflate. Exhaustion clouds his face, his eyes heavy as he nods. "Let's hear it, then. We can't afford to lose this chance."

I recite the list we agreed on. Most of it is simple things, like more torches and double the order of food—even though I reminded him I couldn't hope to eat enough to require doubling the food—but some of it is the type of demands one might expect of a king. I told him silk bed sheets were too obviously for me and not him, but he does demand wine to drink and books for me to read to him.

Prince Noctere raises an eyebrow. "How lucky for him we sent a servant who can read."

"He asked, and I told him I could," I say, which isn't entirely untrue, as we had the conversation well over a year ago. "He says he misses stories."

"Well, stories are all he'll ever have, so I suppose we can spare some damn books. And some soldiers to help you carry it all over."

I bite my lip for a moment, debating. I've gotten what I was sent for, and now we'll at the very least have enough to eat and torches to light the cell. But I look at the prince who once felt like my friend, who has threatened me with the front lines, and take yet another risk.

"What does this mirror do?" I ask, then hasten to explain. "He's reluctant, your highness, so maybe, I thought, if I knew, I could—I don't know. Convince him of the greater purpose, perhaps."

Maybe I could. Maybe I could convince him to give me the mirror. Maybe I could convince him to see things Prince Noctere's way.

If only Prince Noctere can convince me, first.

"From what I understand, my uncle is immune to the concept of a greater purpose," he says. That doesn't sound true at all to me, but I don't argue.

"I'll tell you this story quickly. It's not a story for public consumption, but why not? I already know you can keep your mouth shut."

I suppress my wince at that, but he's not wrong, so I just listen.

"The mirror was a fable, essentially. But my uncle used to have a talent, we'll say, for finding items. He liked the research and he liked the hunt. The more powerful, or dangerous, or obscure, the better. So he went after the mirror."

"But what does it do?" I press. "Your highness?"

"The mirror is enchanted to show you at your most powerful. If you can look into it, you might see the path to obtaining power for yourself."

The pieces of this story begin to make sense. Why it was such a divisive element in our nation's history. Why Prince Noctere wants it, and why King Osir doesn't think he should give it up.

I wish I could say Prince Noctere could be trusted with it, but I'm beginning to understand King Osir's thought that no one can be.

What isn't clear is what exactly happened when King Osir found it. He was imprisoned over the mirror, and I'd always heard he'd murdered several of his brothers and several hundred humans before he was finally imprisoned. What did he see in the mirror that led to that?

How can a man see his most powerful self and somehow immediately end up imprisoned under the earth for a century?

Prince Noctere leans forward in his chair. "We need that mirror, Leana. It could make the difference in this war."

I nod, studying him, with bags under his eyes and skin almost as pale and pinched as his father. He'd always looked more like his mother than his father, but this threat of war is bringing out the worn-down look his father always had.

We think of him as a prince, as a dragon, as a fierce and formidable creature. But the truth is that Prince Noctere is barely older than me. And this kingdom has been left for him to shoulder alone for too long.

"You look tired," I venture, unsure of my welcome but needing to say it, anyway.

We were friends, once. Does he ever think about that?

"War is tiring," he says simply, brushing me off. "Find me a way to end it, Leana. That's your job. Leave me with everything else." He stands, and I do too. "You'll have your supplies within the hour. Don't disappoint me, please."

There's a threat lingering under his words, but I hear the desperation, too.

CHAPTER TEN

OSIR

I actually enjoy arguing with my mate over the items I send her to the castle for. She rejects several of the items out of hand. First tremulously, like she can't believe she would contradict me, but gaining confidence when nothing bad happens to her.

I confess that by the end, I add ridiculous items to the list on purpose, just to try to hear her argue with me more, just so she can see that she can argue without consequence.

My little mate is a queen who has been told she's inconsequential for too long. And that stops now. She will learn to argue and demand and present her perspective and make others listen, especially when she knows she's right.

Even if I'm still upset that she refuses to demand a proper bed for this cell, I'm proud of her for sticking to her convictions.

A proper mate would be able to kiss their treasure goodbye before a journey, but a dragon's mouth should go nowhere near my mate, so I refrain, just telling her to be careful and come back to me.

I listen to her footfalls all the way out of the cave, and then am left in darkness and silence. The natural state of my world for a century feels like it's choking me after just one day of her presence. But I have to push myself beyond that.

I need a plan. We can't trick the prince forever.

***

I'm no closer to a solution to our problem as the day passes. My mate could perhaps steal a key to my chains, but I'd be foolish to count on that. Most likely, the key was long ago melted down and re-forged into something else, and even if it wasn't, they would never give her access to it.

I could try to bargain with my nephew, offer to win his war for him, and seat him on the throne. I would get some sick pleasure in dethroning my brother, but then I'd be left an outcast dragon with no throne, no home, and a mate to care for. It's not an impossible situation, but it wouldn't allow me to show my treasure how she should be treated, so it gets moved to the bottom of my list.

And there's still the option of convincing Leana to run away, to vanish and take my hoard with her to secure her future. The thought alone hurts, but my needs shouldn't be the driving force behind my decisions. If I thought I could convince Leana to do it, I would, and damn the consequences to myself.

It's still a viable plan, and I keep it in mind. I will send her away from me forever. I will accept my lot of rotting under this earth, if it means she will be safe and free to live a life.

I think of the day a century ago where I found the mirror, where I eagerly looked into it. I'd cracked the frame slightly with my strength and eagerness, but it hadn't affected the glass any. I could still see the future before me, clear as anything.

And the future was a world aflame. The light in the mirror was so bright I couldn't hope to see anything else. That's the kind of flame that could burn away chains and this hole in the ground and my brother and an entire invading army.

It's a kind of flame brighter than any dragon I've ever heard of being able to wield, unnaturally bright. If it showed up in the mirror, then it must mean I'll find it within me someday. But it's been a century, and I still have no idea how to summon that type of fire.

I hear the grate creaking open, and then footsteps, shaking me from my thoughts. I can pick out Leana's steps even from here, even over the absolutely thundering noise of whoever is following her, and I listen with pleasure as she draws closer.

At last, Leana emerges into my cavern, flames wreathing her skin and casting her in an absolute, mouth-watering glow.

I'm suddenly struck with the thought that the biggest crime against me isn't keeping me from my kingdom, my wealth, or the sky. It's keeping me in this form so I can't properly show my mate what it would mean to please her. Because right now, I desperately ache to please her.

"You've returned," I say simply, knowing there are ears listening just outside of my sight.

She smirks at me, a smile I haven't seen before. Conspiratorial, I would call it, and it makes the fire in my belly burn a little brighter. Because she and I are a team, us against them.

"I've returned with your demands, your majesty," she says. "Give me a moment to bring them to you."

"Surely they sent you assistants to carry it all?"

"Your nephew wanted to make sure you had what you wanted," she says. "Four soldiers accompanied me to carry it all here. But they don't wish to come in."

I don't particularly wish to see them either, but I can't resist. I raise my volume. "You are all such cowards that you'd send a mere girl to face me when you cannot?"

No one moves, and I want to laugh. Of course, my treasure would show more bravery than every soldier in this kingdom.

I sniff deeply. At least one of them is a dragon. Even so, he's unwilling to face me, when here I am, chained to the earth, a century out of practice.

My treasure faced me with bravery, even before she knew I would never dream of hurting her.

Leana smiles again, a private one, just for me, because we're in on this joke together, and my heart swells. "It'll be just a moment, your majesty," she says, loud enough for the soldiers to hear, and she takes the opportunity to bow to me—cheeky girl—before going to bring in pack after pack.

She starts producing items, books and wine and plentiful food—mostly meat, I realize, so unlike what I've been given for the last century. "Is it what you wanted?" she asks me quietly, and I can hear that she's asking for our audience, but also as a genuine question for me.

Is it what I wanted? I couldn't care less about what I have for me, and unfortunately, all this serves me more than it serves her. I want comforts for my mate.

Maybe my nephew would understand such a thought, dragon to dragon, but I can hardly tell him. I can't give him that leverage over me.

I don't know him. Would he hurt Leana to get the mirror from me? His father was certainly willing to do worse.

I hear feet shuffling right outside my cavern and tilt my head. "Is there more?"

"No, that's the last of it. I believe Prince Noctere told them to wait for your answer."

"My answer?"

"The mirror, your majesty." She stands there watching me, head tilted slightly, waiting to see what I do.

Right, the damned mirror. I want to ask her what lies she told my nephew about my cooperation, but now is hardly the time. First, I need to get rid of our audience.

I pull myself up to my full height. Those soldiers can't see it, but it hardly matters. Being a king is about voice, and projecting just right. "I didn't make this deal to immediately give up my leverage. Once your supposed prince proves to me that the supplies will keep coming, then perhaps we can talk."

The soldiers in the hallway keep shuffling around. I huff. There was once a time when such a proclamation would have sent people scrambling, but apparently no more.

Oh well. There are other ways to get my point across. I blow a stream of fire over my treasure's head and wait for them to get my point.

They do, and I listen as their feet scramble over the rocks, beginning the arduous climb out of my prison.

Leana and I can't speak freely while they still linger in here, so I take the opportunity to watch her, taking in the sight of her, ensuring no harm came to her while she was out of my sight.

She looks well, if tired. My first instinct is to encourage her to sit down, to relax after her long day, but I suppose I can't say anything before the soldiers leave.

She takes the time to organize the supplies she brought in, setting food to one side and books to another. A smear of grease ends up on her tunic and she frowns. "Should have asked for a cake of soap," she says quietly. "I'll have to wash this eventually."

I should have had her ask for the finest clothes that could be found on short notice, clothes fit for a queen. And I would say so, but my mind is stuck on her washing the only outfit she has. Or bathing. She'll want to bathe eventually, too. And as far as I know, the only water down here is the slowly bubbling spring in this cavern that I drink from.

The grate creaks closed above us, the faint click my ears have become so accustomed to. "They're gone." Leana's shoulders relax. "Eat," I urge her. "You must be hungry."

She climbed this cavern five times in just the last few days, and I doubt they thought to feed her at the castle.

"Do you even drink wine?" she asks me, and I'm pleased to hear that she's dropped the titles now that our audience is gone.

"Never in this form. But there might be a first time for everything." Dragons aren't particularly known for our fine control in this form, or even our sense of taste. A fine wine

80

seems wasted on a creature that would as soon eat a cow raw. "What did you learn at the castle, Leana?"

She doesn't answer for a long moment, busying herself with the books, but I wait. "I think your brother is dying," she says eventually.

Well, that's somewhat unexpected. I had wondered why she talks so much about this nephew of mine and not my brother, but that might explain it. "How do you know?"

She shrugs. "Prince Noctere seems restless. Driven in a way that I can't explain. He's overwhelmed with this all. And I already knew no one has seen the king in months."

I want to protest her calling that piece of shit a king, but I refrain, focused instead on the information. His mate. It's the only explanation. Braxil is far too young to naturally be succumbing to death.

Dragons mate for life, and we do not say that lightly. Once a commitment is made, the bond is eternal. Without a mate, a dragon might live a thousand years or more. With a mate, if both are properly cared for? The upper limit is significantly higher. Maybe it doesn't exist.

But only dragons mate for life. We can never leave our mates, but humans can leave us and reject our bond. It can be devastating for both sides, and always cuts their life force short.

I'm sure my brother was a fool about it. I'm sure he shamed or even hurt her in some way, and I wouldn't blame her for leaving him.

She must be suffering now, though. If my brother is really dying, then she must be too.

I don't explain this to Leana. I am not so far gone, so desperate, that I would tell my mate that my lifespan is significantly shorter than expected if she doesn't accept me. That I will die the day she does unless she lets me give her eternal life, at the price of an eternal commitment.

That would be coercion of the worst order, because I know my treasure, and she might be foolish and give in against her own wishes to take care of me. And if the worst comes to pass, if I fail her as a mate and she gets sent off to war, then I won't have her worrying about me when she'll need to worry about herself first.

So I keep my thoughts to myself. "So we have an inexperienced leader going to a war he's not ready for, seeking a magical artifact he can't hope to understand to help him," I surmise. "You said my nephew was a child when you were?"

She nods. Still so young, then. Especially for a dragon.

"The prince and I, we were friends," she says. "Or as friendly as a royal can be with a servant. My mother served his mother, and came all the way from her home kingdom with her. So I was a good way to keep him entertained when our mothers were busy."

There is something dark lurking there. "What happened?" I ask as gently as I can.

"He almost killed my mother," she says slowly, making me jolt. "And then his mother left."

Chapter Eleven

LEANA

I've never had to tell anyone this story. After all, the prince's weaker moments growing up weren't meant to be publicly declared, so I'd long ago learned to keep everything from that time to myself.

But King Osir isn't just someone I've met. I'm not spreading gossip. I'm speaking to a king, and he needs to know.

I tell myself that, at least. Maybe it's just the way his soft words and his focused eyes always make me want to tell him everything.

"We were young," I say, thinking back to that day. I'd been missing my two front teeth still, I think. We were young enough that catching frogs had sounded like a suitable afternoon pursuit. "My mother gave him a command on behalf of his mother. He was supposed to go inside and get clean.

Someone he was meant to impress was coming by and he needed to be a prince, not a little boy. And he didn't want to go."

"So he tried to kill your mother?" he demands, nostrils flaring as he speaks.

I decide not to ask about all the humans he supposedly killed. Instead, I shrug. "Tried puts it strongly. I think he was just young and out of control and threw a tantrum. Unfortunately, his tantrums contained fire. And my mother..." I shake my head.

The flames had been sudden and unexpected. One minute I was waiting in the mud beside him, waiting to see if we'd go back to our games or I'd lose my companion for the rest of the day. The next I'd been lunging for my mother, instinct compelling me in a way I couldn't understand.

"Your mother?" he prompts.

"I dove in front of her. I didn't know what I could do yet. I'd been able to light a finger on fire, but no more than the head of a candle. But I didn't think. I ran, and I got hit, and it's like the fire just disappeared inside of me."

And over a decade later, it convinced the prince I was an appropriate jailor for his uncle. Someone he wouldn't be able to burn.

We hadn't spoken at all between the frog-catching day and the day I was pulled aside and sent to feed King Osir.

Our friendship—companionship, more like, presented to each other by circumstances rather than any legitimate want on our own part—had ended that day. Gone were the days of playing tag and hunting for frogs and him confiding in me his frustrations with his father and his lessons and court protocol. I became a servant, as nameless and faceless as all the others. He didn't need me anymore.

I'd been a reminder of both our mothers, what he lost and the mistake his fit had caused. I'm sure he wanted to forget.

But now I'm here with his uncle, who is blowing smoke out of his nostrils.

"You survived. It didn't hurt you?"

"Not at all," I tell him. "It tingles. I can stick my arm in a kitchen fire and be just fine. It's little pinpricks, perhaps, but no more."

"Fascinating," he breathes. "How did Braxil react?"

"He was a little preoccupied. His wife left the next night, in the middle of the night."

He swallows. "Yes, that would preoccupy him. So that's how my nephew knew you couldn't be hurt by me."

"Yes."

I always hate thinking about that day. Not because I'm scared of fire, because I'm not. I didn't know it then, but I wasn't ever in any real danger. But that day changed everything for me, and it always feels bitter and cold.

I'd never heard from my mother again after she left.

It hits me then that the child, the one whose temper tantrum almost killed my mother and I, two innocent humans, will be king. And if I'm right, he'll be king soon, with an oncoming war.

"I really think your brother might be dying."

He huffs. "Probably. And that stupid princeling will take his place."

I raise an eyebrow. "You don't know him."

"I can guess enough."

"Could you help him?" I hesitantly ask. It's not my place to offer suggestions to kings, but I can't forget the way he let me argue with him earlier.

His tail flicks. Not a positive sign, then. "Perhaps. If he'd accept help. But I won't do it for nothing."

"What would you do it for?" I ask after a moment, after realizing that he's entertaining my suggestion. I blush, looking down. This is the second time today he's listened to me like this.

He tilts his head and looks at me for a long moment. "For our future," he simply says.

I know what he means. For his freedom.

Oh, he probably wants other things as well. He's a dragon; I've never known them to pass up riches and luxury. But at the heart of it, he means freedom.

Should he be freed? He keeps talking about it like it's a foregone conclusion, but now I feel like I'm encouraging it.

Osir has been locked up for a century. And while he seems so innocent and kind when he's speaking to me, I have to remind myself of what he did.

He killed his brothers. He killed humans, probably hundreds of them. He was deemed dangerous and locked beneath the earth so he could never hurt anyone ever again. And as much as he's tugged at my heart these past few years, the decision was made for a reason.

Would any of that matter anymore if he could end this war? If he could help the prince and stabilize the kingdom?

And where do I fit into this? He said our future. He keeps talking about our future, what we will do, what he'll give me when he's free.

"Do you want me to go get the prince?" I ask, fully knowing that I'm crossing some line. "I think I could convince him to come here."

Dragons don't show physical discomfort the same way humans do, in my experience. For Noctere to have such significant bags beneath his eyes, I have to believe the pressure has been immense. I wonder if he even sleeps at all anymore. If I could bring him a solution, even if it isn't the one he originally wanted, surely he'd need to listen.

Osir's tail flicks again. "Not yet," he says. "He'll likely just ask for that stupid mirror."

I bite my lip, but ultimately decide to just say it. He hadn't forbidden me from getting more information, or told me the topic was off-limits, after all. "He told me the mirror shows you at your most powerful."

"Not quite. The mirror is an oracle, like the name suggests," he explains, and his tone takes on an almost scholarly approach. He doesn't react at all to me having acquired more information, just slips into explaining. I remember Noctere told me that he used to hunt down artifacts and myths, and wonder about the human form of Osir. Would he look like one of the professors in the castle libraries? One of Noctere's tutors from our childhood?

"And as an oracle, if you jump through the right hoops, the mirror will show you how you can become powerful. But like most oracles, the answer isn't incredibly straightforward." His tail flicks again.

"What did you see?" I ask. It's an incredibly bold question, one I don't think I would have dared to ask yesterday.

But if he's surprised I asked, he doesn't show it. "Fire," he says slowly. "So much fire."

The air feels thick and soupy between us, like I'm swimming through the tension. "Is that why you…" I hesitate, trailing off, not sure how I could possibly ask what I want to know.

He understands my question anyway. "No," he says shortly. "That was… no. Not the same fire."

I don't dare ask anymore. I don't know what I fear more: that he'll answer, or that he won't.

Chapter Twelve

OSIR

Someday, and probably soon, I'm going to have to tell my mate the entire horrific story of how I ended up in this cell. Of the terrible things I did, the mistakes I made.

But it won't be right now.

I briefly entertain what I'll do if she asks. Would I deny her, my mate, my greatest treasure? Would I dare?

She doesn't ask, and I don't have to answer that question. Not yet, at least.

Instead, she turns back to organizing our supplies, picking up fresh torches to set them around our space. With a quick snap of her fingers, she lights them, and I watch her fire.

It burns bright. Dragon fire almost always burns red, and I've always thought Leana's does too. But the edges are almost white, I realize, completely captivated by watching her.

I want to feel her fire. I want it to lick at my skin, to find the softest part of my scales and leave a permanent reminder of her presence in my life.

I'm halfway to asking her to do it before I remember that asking that would be foolish. It would push her far further than she's comfortable with.

Leana is my mate, my greatest treasure, but right now she barely trusts me, and I need to remember that.

"Eat with me?" I ask her. Sharing a meal is always a good place to start, I suppose.

She brings over a chicken, ripping off a drumstick for herself and holding out the rest for me. I take it, careful not to let my claws touch her. I don't want to scare her.

A dragon with a human mate should get to court them in human form. They should get to choose when to show them the dragon form, when they know the human will believe that the form is their protector and not a monster meant to hurt them. They shouldn't be forced to show the human only the scariest parts of themselves.

What stories has she heard about these claws? I don't have another way to approach her, but I desperately wish I did.

She doesn't flinch, though. I take that as a victory.

"Drink some of the wine," I tell her. "I'm certainly not going to."

"Why did you ask for it, then?" she asks. She's not complaining, precisely, but she is definitely close. And as much as I wish that I never would cause my treasure to complain, I hope to hear it more.

She's getting more comfortable with me. She hasn't tried to use a title except when we had an audience. She debated with me. She's asking me things and even complaining.

She trusts me.

"They'd expect a king to ask for wine," I say. "Kings and dragons are both creatures prone to fits of luxury. And when one is both, it can get positively outlandish." I look down at the bottles, peering at the labels. I don't recognize the names of the vineyards marked on them, but perhaps that's not surprising after a century.

"Bring some closer, I'll tell you which ones are worth drinking," I tell her. It's been a century, but I know I can still smell the difference between good wine and cheap swill.

She obediently brings me three bottles, and I carefully lower my head towards her. She doesn't flinch, and I sniff each bottle carefully.

"None of these are good enough for you," I proclaim, flicking my tail. It's the type of wine you serve to fourth-rate castle guests you're forced to entertain, not to a future queen.

She puts two of the bottles down and looks at the third, shrugging. "I've never had more than a few sips before, so I won't know the difference."

"Never?"

"When would you imagine I would?" she responds. "Servants don't go to parties. Or at least, not to drink the wine." She struggles with the cork, but gets it open after a moment.

Then I watch her drink directly from the bottle, taking two long sips, her head thrown back, the column of her throat working as she swallows.

Oh, to be in human form and able to touch that throat. Press kisses into it, cradle it with a hand, hold her and show her my devotion with every touch.

I want to press kisses to her neck after I've draped it in jewels. I want to fasten her necklace for her and kiss her skin when I finish.

All of these dreams require being out of this prison.

"Slow down," I advise her. "If you really haven't had more than a few sips before, this will be overwhelming."

She lowers the bottle. "You sure you don't want some?"

I hold up one giant, clawed hand—or what passes as a hand on a dragon, anyway. "I don't think I can maneuver the bottle," I admit.

Shoving a chicken in my mouth is one thing. I don't care if it ends up mutilated and pricked full of claw marks first. But I don't think I can manage a glass wine bottle.

She smiles at me, soft and light in a way that makes my breath catch. So soft. So open. I've never seen such a smile from her before, and I half wonder if the wine is already hitting her. But no, it can't be.

She's just feeling this way. Soft, and generous, and open. And it's towards me. It makes something new and unfamiliar build inside me.

"Come here," she says, gesturing me down towards her with the hand not holding the wine bottle.

"What?"

"Bend down. Bring your head closer to me."

I have no idea what she wants, but I'm hardly going to disobey the first order my mate gives me. I move slowly, not because I don't want to follow her command, but because I'm still worried about frightening her.

My head is bigger than her entire body, but she doesn't so much as twitch when I lower my head beside her.

"Open," she says, and I obediently open my mouth.

She tips the bottle slowly, giving me a taste of the wine. It's wasted on a dragon, I'm sure, but it's sweeter than anything I've tasted in a century.

But it wouldn't be half as sweet as her.

I'd like to blame the wine for the direction my thoughts have taken, but that would be a lie. I can't stop thinking about it.

A dragon is blessed with two forms. One to protect their mate, the other to love their mate. And I'm useless even as protection, chained as I am. But I ache to love her like she deserves.

I swallow the sweet wine, the bottle barely being a mouthful for me. "Thank you, treasure."

"Would you like more? There's plenty."

"I'm alright, Leana." My head is already close to her, so I take a risk and lay down around her again, like I did last night. "Did you enjoy your wine?"

She sits down next to me without my prompting and then shifts to rest against me. She's so pleasantly warm in a way I wouldn't expect. No one is ever as warm as a dragon.

She tilts her head, considering my question, and the languid, easy movement tells me the wine she drank is affecting her. "Yes. Thank you for sharing."

I nudge her side gently. "It's not sharing, Leana. It's already yours."

"How can it be mine? I have nothing," she protests, her brow furrowing.

"You're wrong. You have everything I have." I look around ruefully. "It might not look like much right now, but I assure you, it will be."

"You're very confident," she muses, and I would respond, tell her that I have to be, but she nuzzles even closer into my side, and I can't form a single thought other than the heat of her body, the soft weight of her, the mouthwatering alluring shape of her presence.

"Are you tired?" I ask, trying to keep my voice soft, a difficult ask of a creature with a diaphragm the size of most rooms.

"A little bit," she murmurs, and then she turns even deeper into my side. "Do you mind if I sleep here?"

"I want nothing more," I promise her, and then watch in awe as my tiny little human treasure closes her eyes, snuggles into my side, and trusts me to watch over her when she sleeps.

Chapter Thirteen

Leana

I wake up slowly again, warm and relaxed. It likely says something that I've never slept as well as I have in this cave, with a supposedly terrifying dragon wrapped around me.

He's awake when I open my eyes. "Did you sleep?" I ask him, forcing myself to sit up. He really is more comfortable than my bed back at the palace, even with his scratchy scales.

I rub sleep out of my eyes, then feel my hair, half fallen out of its braid. I untie it, letting it fall down. It's not like I have work to do where my hair could get in the way, after all.

"For a bit. Dragons don't need as much sleep in this form," he says.

He's been chained down here for a century with absolutely nothing to do and doesn't even have the ability to just sleep the time away. I feel a pang of misery at that.

It's a punishment, I remind myself. He's a murderer, and he's not supposed to enjoy his time down here.

But I can't convince myself to believe it anymore.

The stories of the mad king justly imprisoned beneath the earth just seem so much less believable when I'm faced with the real man that inspired them.

I look around the cavern. The old torches burned down in the night, so I light my hand, thinking of standing up to light the new ones. Will they last the whole week until we get resupplied?

I rejected Osir's order to leave him when the light runs down, because I'm never truly in the dark and this is the safest place for me right now. But the truth is, I can't imagine actually being left in the dark, so far underground. I worry that it'll feel like suffocating, and I don't want to find out.

Would I leave him if the light ran out? Would I be able to do it? He'd tell me to, of that I have no doubt. But something tells me I wouldn't be able to do it. Not even if he, a king, ordered me to.

I move to stand and Osir huffs. "Where are you going, treasure?"

"I'm going to light fresh torches. Get some light back in here." I stand, and it's ridiculous that I feel colder when I'm not next to him. "Can you see in the dark?"

"Better than you can. Color is leached from the world like that, though." Even with just my flames to light the huge space, I can feel his eyes on me. "And I can't abide a colorless world when you're here to look at."

I feel my face heat with a flush, and I very determinedly turn away from him to contend with the torches.

How does he do it? How does he say such things, things I'd never have believed in a thousand years from anyone else, and make them sound so sincere? I can't doubt him. I couldn't even if I wanted to, and I alarmingly find myself wanting to less and less.

What would it mean to be his mate? To be his treasure, to be at his side? If he really escapes from here, like he pretends he's so confident about, what would that be like?

I set the torches around our space and light them, taking my time to gather my composure. It would be nice to light all of them, to really light up the grim cavern, but I hold almost all of them back, lighting only four, one in each direction. It will be enough light to see, at any rate.

"That's better," Osir rumbles as I finish. "A lovely view." Then he actually stretches, looking once more like the world's largest cat.

"Of course," he continues, "It'd be a better view if I could dress you properly. I'm thinking silk, soft to the touch and delicate. And blue would look marvelous against your skin. Or red, perhaps, like the fire in your soul. And jewels, of course. I'll have you positively dripping."

"What is your obsession with giving me jewels?"

"You are a treasure who deserves treasure," he says promptly, like it's an obvious thought.

I look at my clothes. I've worn them for multiple days now, and the grease stain from the chicken last night is the least of my concerns. I've climbed in and out of this cave multiple times, sat in the dirt, cleaned rooms, and made the rather hot and sweaty walk back and forth to the castle.

Me, in silk? It's a ludicrous thought.

He must see it on my face, because he asks, "Have you ever considered why dragons keep hoards?"

"Dragons like to collect things, I thought."

"I suppose we do. But mostly, dragons keep hoards for their mates. Our mate is the pinnacle of our treasures. The most desired, the most beloved. And nothing will ever give a dragon greater satisfaction than seeing their mate adorned in and enjoying the lesser treasures of their hoard."

His voice takes on a wistful quality as he talks about it, like the thought of draping me in silk really is his dearest wish, and I can't help but to think about it.

He huffs a great, heaving sigh, and I watch him eye the piles of food, wine, and books. "And I've presented a rather poor hoard for you."

For now, I almost say, then catch myself. Apparently, his belief that we'll not only escape but actually begin a life together here is starting to influence my thoughts.

"Would you like me to read to you?" I ask instead, hoping to distract us both. "Since you asked for all these books." And since we have nothing better to do, I don't say.

I briefly remember that I actually have a job, that I was sent here for a reason. That I'm supposed to be extracting information from the fallen king.

I dismiss the thought.

His eyes brighten at my suggestion, and he lifts his head. "Yes, please. Pick whichever book looks most interesting to you; I'm not fussy."

That seems untrue to me. But I remember that Noctere said he liked stories and myths. Perhaps he truly does just miss books.

So I find a book of children's fairy stories. "This one?" I ask, holding it up for him to read the title.

"Bring a bottle of wine. Or two," is all he says.

I do as he asks, curling up against his side again, and letting the warmth seep into my bones.

***

We're halfway through the fourth bottle of wine when I misjudge a pour into his waiting mouth and accidentally spill wine, splashing it all over my arm and tunic.

"Damn it," I curse, but the bite of it is taken out by the wine. It's all under a slight haze, like the world is just so slightly out of focus.

Osir lets out a sound that I think might be a tsk. "When those useless soldiers come back, I'm demanding better clothes for you. Damn what they think of it," he says.

I clumsily try to pat the wine dry. "I suppose I'll just smell like a drunk until then."

"Don't be silly, treasure. You should bathe."

I nod, feeling a smile tug at my face that I can't fight, the idea seeming more funny than it perhaps should be. "Ah, yes. Of course. Can you point me in the direction of the bathing chamber?"

Is it the wine or the way he looks at me that makes me comfortable making such a sarcastic comment? Perhaps it's a bit of both.

"I'm afraid I don't have much to present to you, but there's the spring right over there," he says, gesturing to the spring just at the edge of the reach of his chains.

"That's the drinking water," I protest.

"There's a bucket," he says, and I must imagine the droop in his posture when he says this. "It's not ideal, perhaps, but you can at least clean yourself and wash your clothes."

I stare at him, something about the moment cutting through the haze of the wine. "I'd need to..." I can't finish my thought.

What does it matter if I'm naked? It's not like it would inspire anything in particular to happen. Not with him in this form.

And I've been naked in front of others before. Yes, they were fellow servants, and always female, and we'd been too focused on ourselves in the usually freezing-cold water to notice much. But I had done it before. I could do it again.

Would it even be that different?

CHAPTER FOURTEEN

OSIR

If I was a kind dragon, a good person, I would suggest she fill the bucket and move to the part of the cave outside my cavern where I wouldn't be able to see her. That's where she's been going to handle the need for a toilet, after all—far more dignified than me simply having to bury it and both of us having to act like she doesn't notice—and it would be a sufficient amount of privacy.

If I was a good dragon, I would promise her I wouldn't look. And, more importantly, I would mean it.

I can't make myself make the promise. Not unless she asks for it. I'll follow my treasure's commands, but I find myself unable to offer it of my own free will.

I try to think of how to comfort her, but then she squares her shoulders. "Alright, then. That sounds like a good idea."

I watch eagerly as she walks over to the spring, bucket in hand, wondering what she's thinking. Is she nervous? Or is she excited?

Or perhaps I'm a sex-starved old dragon desperate for my mate, and Leana is simply concerned with getting clean, and I should leave her in peace.

She submerges the bucket, pulling up a frankly pathetic amount of water. If I had my way, she'd have a bath big enough for half a dozen, and it would always be hot, although I suppose she and I could adequately warm a bath on our own. There'd be shelf upon shelf of every soap and bath oil she could ever dream of.

There wouldn't be any bath attendants, though. That role, I could more than eagerly fill.

I watch with rapt attention as she raises gently trembling hands to her waist, lifting the tunic over her head and setting it aside.

All I can see is her bare back, muscled from her manual labor.

Muscled and tense looking. If only I had human hands. I've never given anyone a massage, but I'm sure I could figure it out. The warmth of a dragon's hands would be soothing, surely.

There's no clean cloth or cake of soap, so she makes do with just her hand and the water, cupping it onto her skin, letting it run across her frame before briskly rubbing.

What I wouldn't give to be the one rubbing her skin.

Then get free, you foolish, stupid dragon, I scold myself. The answer to all our problems lies with that one action.

And then the thought is driven out of my head when she turns sideways, just enough for me to see her in profile.

Her hair is covering most of her face, so my greedy eyes trail lower to her small, pert breasts. I desperately wish to suck at them, squeeze them, to see if she wants that as badly as I do.

I force myself to keep silent. I won't frighten her. My purpose is to treat her like the treasure she is, not intimidate her.

I trail my eyes across the rest of her body, stomach that could do with some fattening leading to lush hips that would cradle my human form perfectly. Her hips and the treasure that lies between them are still tantalizingly hidden by her trousers, and I am desperate, nearly feral, for her to take them off.

She finishes sloshing water along her torso, then dumps the last dregs of the bucket before drawing more water. I lean slightly closer, unable to help myself, eager to see what she'll do next.

Except she doesn't reach for her trousers. Instead, she reaches for her tunic, and I can't help myself.

I tell myself it's because I don't want her to undo her hard work. It's not simply because I'm staring like a lecherous old king.

"You'll get yourself all dirty again," I tell her.

She jumps, then turns to me, inadvertently giving me a perfect view. Her breasts bounce with the movement, and I think about other, more pleasurable activities we could be doing to make her breasts bounce.

"You were watching," she says, and there's accusation in her voice, but, all things considered, it sounds rather mild. Perhaps it's the wine, although I don't think she had more than would fill a few glasses. Perhaps she just doesn't mind me watching that much.

Perhaps, the lecherous old king inside me whispers, she even likes it.

"I was," I agree, because I won't lie to her. "You'll get yourself dirty again if you put that on before washing it."

She sighs and then submerges the tunic in the bucket of water, lifting it out to squeeze it out before repeating the process. When she holds it up again, she has a slightly stained, soaking wet tunic.

"You'll catch your death if you put that on."

"Do you have alternate clothes hidden somewhere?" she asks, testy now, and I spare a moment to be proud that she'd speak to me this way.

"If I had my way, I would," I point out to her, which doesn't seem to please her very much. "I promise, Leana. I mean you no harm. Get clean. Treat this space like it's yours. Tell me what will make you comfortable," I say, knowing very well she could tell me to close my eyes. And if she does, I'll do it. Only a fool doesn't obey their queen.

She sighs, a deep exhale that makes her shoulders droop. Then she walks shirtless to a large rock, spreading her tunic out on it as best she can.

"I don't... I've never..." she says, half-turning to me, and I know what she means.

"I won't hurt you," I say, trying to gentle my voice as much as possible. "I won't touch you, either, Leana." Not by choice, maybe, but perhaps for once it's better that the decision is taken from my hands.

She actually gives me a small smile, one that lodges deep inside me. "I'm not worried about that."

She's not? Because she knows these chains hold me, or she trusts me?

I could reach her, although I'd never approach my mate with dragon claws. The spring is within my limited range of mobility. She has to know that.

She trusts me.

"Then what worries you, treasure?" I ask, keeping my voice as calm as I possibly can, even when my heart beats faster than I can ever remember it beating.

She shrugs, walking back towards the spring. "I've just never done this before."

I swallow. "Never?" I'd suspected, but to hear it confirmed...

"I've bathed in a river with other servants. But never on purpose, if you understand. And I know you're telling me to just get clean, but you're not watching to make sure I'm clean."

"No, treasure, I'm not." To make sure she's clean? If I had my way, if I was free and I had a castle with a soft bed to lay her in, I'd make us both very, very dirty. And then bathe her myself, gently, sensuously, just so we could get filthy again.

The fantasy is a nice one, but I'm more focused on the vision before me. She begins to lower her trousers, and I find myself holding my breath.

It all comes rushing out in one long groan, powerful enough to shake rocks, as she tosses the trousers aside to address after, her beautiful body on full display. "Good gods, treasure. Nothing has ever been more beautiful."

She looks down at herself. "Me?"

"Yes, you," I say, eying her beautiful cunt that she's likely inadvertently giving me an excellent view of. With curls of midnight black, I long to part her lips enough to see the wet, pink flesh hidden underneath.

I'd be the first to touch it. That thought sends a bolt of lust through me.

Our dragon forms are never meant to be our lusty forms, and feelings like lust are slightly muted in this form, like they're behind a wall, just out of sight.

If this is muted, she is going to bring me to my knees the minute I'm free.

She dismisses my lust so easily, turning away, back to the bucket. "I'm nothing special."

"You are beauty personified," I tell her, now getting a view of her ass that could stop my heart. "You are the finest treasure in my hoard, a mate beyond what any could ever hope for."

She has the gall to laugh at that. It sounds nervous, and it just makes me ache. "Why do you keep saying things like this?"

"Do you think they're untrue?" I demand, and I can't fight it any longer. I move as far as my chains will allow me, lying on my belly and putting myself right in her space. "Treasure, do you think I'm a liar?"

"I think you tell me very flattering things," she hedges.

"I tell you nothing but the truth. If the truth flatters you, I can't help that." I eye her hungrily, hoping she can see it in my eyes. That she can know it's true.

This moment feels monumental. Like right here, eyeing her naked form, I can convince my mate of her worth. Like I can finally make Leana understand.

If I don't handle this correctly, I fear I could chase her away.

"If I were free, and I had a body built to touch yours, I would make you feel things beyond your wildest imagination," I proclaim.

Now I'm bragging, but it remains true. I'm not unfamiliar with how to pleasure a partner, and my Leana will find that I'm a particularly diligent student for anything I don't already know.

She blushes. "That wouldn't be hard," she tells me, focusing on washing her leg. "I find I have a weak imagination when it comes to such things. I've never..." She can't make herself say it. "All I know is what I've heard from others, in passing. And that never sounded very good."

Servant girls in a castle where my brother had been denied his mate for years? I shudder to think what she might have heard. "It would be so good between us, treasure," I promise her, my voice barely coming out as a rasp. "I swear it would be."

She shivers, and something tells me it's not just her nakedness or the cool water on her skin. She might not know much about what I'm promising her, but I can tempt her. She's interested.

Something feral and entirely beastly warms my insides. It's time to convince my mate that I'm worth it.

Chapter Fifteen

Leana

He's looking at me like he wants to eat me, and yet I've never been more sure that he won't hurt me.

I've long ago abandoned any ideas of this sort of thing. I have no time to meet people, and I've heard stories that make my insides curdle. I've taken the protection offered by being able to light anyone who hurts me on fire and avoided everything having to do with this.

Only now, Osir is lying next to me, offering it in such a sensual, enticing package that it sends shivers through me. My nipples pebble, and I highly doubt it's the chilly air causing that.

He's a dragon. Even if he was in his human form, that fact alone should scare me. Dragons hurt humans. But even as I try to remind myself of that, I can't make it stick in my mind.

Sometime in the last few days, he's gone from his majesty, King Osir, the fallen mad king, to just Osir.

To my dragon, and I immediately try to quash that thought.

But even so, he's not in his human form. I've never seen him in his human form. How can I be feeling like this over a dragon? Is it really just his voice? The sincerity of it, the promises he makes me?

It is, and I find myself wanting to believe him more and more with every moment that passes.

I wash my other leg, forcing myself to work up the courage to say, "Tell me."

His rumble makes the whole cavern shake when I finally say it. "With pleasure," he rasps, eyeing me hungrily. "I've thought about it every day since the day you first walked in here."

"You have not," I protest.

"I absolutely have," he argues. "Every day. I knew the moment you walked in here that you were mine, Leana."

"You didn't say anything."

"I offered you my food every time I saw you, treasure," he rumbles. "And I offered you my hoard."

"How was I supposed to know that meant this?" I demand.

"I admit I don't know much about humans," he says slowly. "I might have missed something. But you're here now, bare and so beautiful, and I cannot stop thinking of how I'm going to treat you when I'm free."

My breath catches. "And how will you treat me?" I dare to ask.

Every time he says it, it sounds less like a fantasy and more like a promise, and I want to hear his promises.

"Like the treasure you are," he says lowly. "Come sit with me if you're done, Leana."

I raise an eyebrow. "I'm naked."

"And your clothes are wet, but I'll stop you from catching a chill," he promises. "I swear on my life, Leana. I would never hurt you."

"I know." I do, too. There's no question in my mind. Osir would never deliberately hurt me.

"Then come sit with me. Let me bask in your presence. I'll keep my hands to myself."

I almost stupidly tell him I don't want him to do that, before I remember his hands end with razor-sharp claws the size of my arm.

So I sit next to him, and he curls up around me, letting me lean against his snout while his shoulder comes to support my back.

And then he takes a great, obvious inhale. "You like what I'm saying, don't you, treasure? You're intrigued." He sounds pleased when he says it.

"How can you tell?"

"I can smell it," he announces. "The sweetest scent I've ever smelled, and if I had my human body, I'd have my face buried between your thighs already, drowning in that scent."

It's so crass. It's so intriguing.

"Really? You'd want that?"

"I will beg you for it, treasure. At least once a day, more if I have my way. You shall be queen and your throne will be my face."

I flush and try to hide my face, but the only place to hide is in his scales.

His tail gently taps me on the hip. "I apologize if I've offended you."

I slowly look up again to find him watching me, attention rapt. I still can't read a dragon's expression, but I think I can tell Osir's tones of voice now, and I think I worried him.

"It's just so crass," I try to explain. "And I'm not used to..." Being crass. Discussing this. Having someone talk about pleasuring me. All are true.

"Crass? Maybe. It's honest. And your pleasure will be so beautiful. I know it. I long for it."

"I don't know anything about this." I understand the fundamentals, I suppose. I've heard more stories than I ever wanted to. I've even stumbled into things I didn't want to see. But when it comes to my own body, I'm far less experienced.

"Let me teach you," he says immediately. "As a dragon until I can do it properly as a man."

I raise an eyebrow at that. "And what does the dragon expect from me?"

"No expectations. But I'd like to watch. That's all."

He wants to watch me. But even with a dragon's predatory eyes, I somehow only ever feel love shining out at me.

Am I a fool for this?

I push the thought aside. Maybe I am. If I am, then I've done a lot of foolish things in the past few days at his urging, and this wouldn't be any more awful, really.

But it does have the possibility of being a lot more pleasurable.

"Tell me."

"I love your breasts," he says immediately. "I've fantasized about them, of course. But today, when you removed that tunic, I want to gaze on them forever."

I look down. "They're not much to look at." I know current court fashion has women in dresses that make their chests look ridiculously large, to a truly fantastic degree. And here I am, with just these little breasts.

"They are enough to bring a man to his knees," he contradicts me. "Will you touch them for me? Show me if they are sensitive?"

I hesitantly run a hand over them, scraping my palm over my pebbled nipple. It doesn't particularly feel like anything, and I frown. Already disappointing him.

"You've never done this before." His tone is neutral, non-judgmental, but I flush again regardless.

"When would I have? In the room I share with three other girls? Or perhaps when bathing in a freezing river?"

"Let me be your guide, then," he offers, although it sounds more like pleading.

"Alright." Just one more foolish thing, then.

"Keep your touch gentle," he tells me. "Slow, light. Just a tease at first. Less is more." His eyes bore into me. "Start at your neck."

Following his directions, I run just the tips of my fingers along my neck, down my throat and to my collarbone. And that touch alone sends shivers through me, like sparks along everywhere I just touched.

"Beautiful," he rasps. "Do it again, and imagine it's my lips."

I shiver again and do as he says, keeping my touch light, a tease, like he said. I'm not sure if it feels anything like lips, but I let my eyes slip closed, picturing it. "Does that feel good, treasure?"

"Mhm." I open my eyes, trying to see him watching me, but he tsks.

"Keep your eyes closed, treasure. All the better to imagine with."

"Alright." I close them again, and, without him prompting, run my fingers further down, scraping along the edge of my breast.

"Good girl. Run it up towards your nipple, now."

I do, keeping the touch just as gentle as he originally told me, and I bite my lip to stop any sound from coming out. That feels unexpectedly good. Like when the fire dances on my skin, like when every nerve feels alive.

"Circle it. And don't bite your lip, treasure. Hearing you will genuinely be the highlight of my century."

A soft gasp comes out at that, and I couldn't stop it if I wanted to. His responding rumble tells me he's enjoying this as much as I am.

"You're so responsive. Perfect girl, my treasure. Now, I think you're ready—pinch your nipple, treasure. It doesn't need to be hard—or maybe it will be. Do whatever feels good."

I pinch, just lightly at first, and it feels like something in my core tightens, something I didn't even know was there. "O-oh."

"Oh, that's a beautiful sound," he says, and his voice almost sounds crooning now. "Can you do that again for me, treasure? Imagine it's my fingers, if it helps."

It does help, somehow. His hands on me, because he wants me—the thought makes that sparking feeling deep, deep inside my core come back.

Would he talk to me as sweetly if I were in bed under him? Would he look at me the same way?

I gasp again, just thinking about it, and his hum of approval tells me perhaps he's thinking of the same thing.

"What-what would you do next?" I manage to ask him, barely recognizing my own voice.

"If I had the honor of having you in bed?" he asks. "I'd keep playing with your nipple if it made you make such lovely sounds. But my mouth would be moving down your body. Touch your stomach, just the fingertips again," he says, and it takes me a minute to process the command, but I obey, shuddering as I feel my own fingers moving down my stomach. "I'm envious of your hand, treasure. It's exactly where I want my mouth to be. Well, not exactly. Not yet." His voice seems to somehow get even lower when he says, "I ache to bury my head between your thighs, Leana. To feast there. To make you come on my tongue, squeezing my head. I can smell you—you're ripe and ready for me and I want to touch you."

I make a sound that sounds more like I've been hurt than anything, although that is the opposite of true. He's smelling me, smelling the wetness I can feel building between my thighs, and I ache to have him touch me there.

I want his hands—his mouth, perhaps his cock—between my thighs. I squeeze my thighs together, feeling how wet he's made me with just my own hand. I won't get him, not today, but every second I'm more and more convinced of his vision of the future. How can I not be? How can I believe in a future where I don't get him?

"What would you do next?" I ask him, trailing my hand to the top of my mound.

His growl shakes his whole body, vibrating through me. It should be terrifying.

It should not make me bite my lip again to hold back a moan. It shouldn't make me even more wet.

"Such a perfect, pretty mate," he croons. "Would you be sweet for me, Leana, and part your thighs? Let them fall open for me?"

I hesitate for just a second and do what he asks, opening my thighs. I keep my own eyes closed so I don't have to look, but I feel his gaze, regardless.

"Beautiful," he rasps. "No dragon has ever been blessed with a prettier mate. None. Trail one finger through your folds, treasure."

I follow his command, feeling the soft, wet flesh part for my finger. "Should I put it inside?" I ask, trailing down to my opening.

"Not yet. Nice and slow, nice and light—bring your finger up higher. Higher—there," he says, clearly seeing the expression on my face when I find the spot he's directing me towards.

I don't need his direction to do it again, gasping as I circle the spot.

"Good girl," he says, noting that I don't need much direction anymore, but giving me his voice. His voice makes whatever it is inside me tighten up almost as much as what I'm doing with my hand, and I don't want him to stop.

"T-tell me," I gasp. "Please. Tell me what you would do."

"Say my name," he says. "Ask with my name and I'll do anything you wish, Leana."

"Osir," I sigh, my head rolling to one side as I keep stroking myself. It's like my strings have been cut, like my muscles can't possibly support me, loose and languid as they are.

Well. All muscles but the ones I can feel tightening inside me.

I didn't know anything could feel this good. I thought this was a thing to be endured, if one was unlucky or wanted children. But here I am, and my dragon king has driven me to such heights with just one of my fingers. "Osir, please, I—" I trail off with a moan, and try to stroke myself the same way again to duplicate the feeling that makes my hips buck slightly.

"Such a perfect mate," he murmurs. "Oh, treasure, if this moment is all I ever get, I will gladly spend a thousand years locked up for it."

I don't like that. I don't want to hear that, not now, not when I can't stop thinking about this future he keeps promising me. "No, we'll get you free," I insist, wanting to open my eyes to argue with him, but he rumbles against me.

"Yes, I must, because my pretty mate wants me to show her how I'd pleasure her, right?" he says. "If ever a man had more incentive to get free... but I'm being rude. I promised I'd help you come if you said my name, and you did, because you're so good for me. It's my turn to keep up my end of the bargain."

I want to touch him. I want his hands on me, his mouth. I know I can't have it, and his scales against my naked skin are a good enough reminder of why. But I still long for it. Ache for it.

"Keep touching yourself, just like you are, good girl," he says. "Is your hand making you feel good?"

"Uh-huh."

"I bet it is. You look delicious, your legs splayed open, your cunt wet and open for me. I'd love to touch you, Leana. I think I'd like more than anything to suck you, suck your sweet little clit into my mouth. And I think you'd like that too, wouldn't you? My tongue, right where your pretty little finger is. And speaking of fingers—once I had you wet and dripping on my face, like the good girl you are, I'd use my finger to slide right inside you. There's a spot inside you that would make you see stars, treasure. Between my finger and my tongue, I'd think I could have you thrashing, ready for release in mere moments."

I bite my lip. "Release?" I ask when I think I can speak without any embarrassing noises.

He hums. "You can feel it now, I imagine. A tightening inside you?"

I hesitate, then nod. "Something... something..."

"Yes," he agrees, clearly hearing through my inadequate explanation. "And it's going to be the most stunning thing I've ever seen. But don't worry about it, Leana. It'll come. Just keep stroking yourself, just like that."

"What about... inside me?" I ask. I know how this works. I know what the purpose of intercourse is.

He hums again. "Do you want something inside you?"

"Do you want to be inside me?" I ask instead of answering.

"Oh, treasure—I want few things more in the entire world. But I would never just shove inside you. I'd be a poor mate if I didn't ensure you were pleasured first."

"Because you being inside me wouldn't pleasure me?" I ask, although I think I know the answer. Surely it must hurt.

He rumbles. "When I'm inside you, treasure, you will feel pleasure like you've never known. I will make you scream for me, beg for more, and I'll give you exactly what you ask for each time, like a good mate. I'm going to make you come first because your pleasure is what I desire most in the world. It's the most erotic thing I can imagine, and I want to watch it."

The raw hunger in his words startles a moan out of me, one loud enough to echo around the cavern. My finger has sped up without my conscious thought, and without him needing to suggest it, I trail my other hand along my throat again, down my collarbone, to my breast once more.

That seems to be all it takes. I feel like a string pulled taut between the two points of pleasure, like some sort of spark has caught. Then the whole string combusts, and I moan his name while something incredible washes through me.

Chapter Sixteen

OSIR

I had half a thought that if there was any force on this earth that could inspire me to spontaneously find the strength to break free of these chains, it would be my mate touching herself right in front of me.

Alas, no such luck regarding the chains, but I can hardly think about them as I watch her come apart.

Her climax is beauty personified. She still has her eyes closed, and her head is thrown back against me as she moans my name, her fingers still working her body as her hips thrust, seeking more.

She didn't like hearing it, but I was right earlier—this one moment would make a thousand years of confinement worth it.

"How do you feel, treasure?" I ask her, watching her come down from her climax. Her legs are still spread, and her eyes are still closed as her head lolls against my scales.

"Sooo good," she mumbles, and pulls her hand from her wet cunt. I watch avidly, eyes torn between watching her slick cunt and her slick fingers.

"I want to taste your fingers more than I want my next breath," I announce before I can think better of it.

She opens her eyes and tilts her head. Just when I think she's about to tell me off, she hesitantly holds out her hand.

I stare at it for a long moment, unable to even think when confronted with the sight. "Were you just saying that? Did you not really want to?" she asks, hesitation creeping into her voice, and I simply can't abide by that.

My too-long lizard tongue darts out, wrapping carefully around her fingers. A dragon's tongue is abrasive, so I'm careful not to drag it over her skin. Still, the moment my tongue makes contact with her slick fingers, my life changes forever.

She's sweet, and if I thought this one taste would be enough, I was sorely mistaken. I want more, desperately. I want to bury my head in her cunt. I want to taste her on my tongue and my fingers. I want to be inside her.

I need to be free.

For me. For her. And not just for this, although my brain cannot hope to think about anything besides her taste right now. No, because my mate deserves to have me fuck her soft and slow in a feathery soft bed. And when she's done, she deserves a warm, relaxing bath.

Speaking of... "I suppose you'll need to wash off again," I say, pulling back and watching her closely.

She doesn't look startled by my closeness. She doesn't even look disturbed by my tongue. No, my mate, my perfect mate, is looking at me through heavy-lidded eyes, and I think perhaps her thoughts line up with my own.

"Is it always like that?" she asks, voice soft.

"It'll only get better," I promise her. I'll show her things she can't even imagine. I'll dedicate every moment of the rest of my long life to her pleasure. I'll give her everything I have to give.

Like jewels, I think with a pang. A thousand jewels, but most prominent whatever that first piece is, the one that will seal our bond forever. I'll choose something worthy of her—a tall order—and she'll accept it, and then I'll shower her with every other piece in my hoard. And she'll look ethereal wearing them, lying back in our bed, with that same heavy-lidded look.

I told myself not to think about that future, about having her be mine, until I had something worthy to offer her. But I can't stop it now. I'm desperate for that future.

***

127

Leana eventually gets up and washes herself off once more, then rinses her trousers. But her clothes are still wet, so I motion her closer to me. "Let me keep you warm," I implore.

She comes to sit where she was before, leaning against my snout and allowing me to wrap around her.

"I don't get cold like normal humans do," she reminds me, but she lets me take more of her weight, regardless.

It's silent for a long moment, and I close my eyes, basking in the feel of her against me.

"What do you get out of that?" she asks me.

"I?" I ask, baffled that she can't already tell. "I get to see my perfect mate come apart."

"And that's it?" she asks, like that's not everything. "What about you? I've been told that men want a certain type of thing, and—"

I cut her off before I can hear what vile thing she's heard about other men. "Whatever they've told you, you deserve far better," I tell her. "You deserve a mate who will treat you like the treasure you are. Who doesn't find any pleasure at all unless you do." I clear my throat, slightly embarrassed to bring up the next part, but she deserves to know anything I know. "And in this form, all those feelings are muted."

She looks at me with alarm. "So I did that and you aren't even feeling those things?"

I try to nudge her by just moving my snout slightly. "I enjoyed every moment," I promise her. "It was the most

128

beautiful thing I've ever seen, and I would watch you touch yourself that way every day for the rest of my life, even if I was never in a position to touch you back. Although, I much rather be able to touch you back," I say, putting as much promise in my voice as I can.

She looks at me with something that seems uncomfortably close to wonder in her dark eyes. "You really mean these things you say to me," she marvels.

"Of course." Was there ever any doubt?

"You really mean it. Ever since the beginning?"

"I have known you were my mate since the moment you first walked in here," I confirm.

She frowns. "You know I'm just a human."

"My mate isn't just anything. She's a human, and a glorious one at that."

"How can you say that? How can you believe that?"

If it wasn't Leana questioning me, I'd be angry. Who would dare question my mate? Who would question her worth, and would dare to do it to my face?

But it is Leana. And I need to parse through what exactly is worrying her, so I can correct it.

"How can I believe that my mate is perfect?" I challenge. "Because you are, treasure, I see you and I know—"

"How can you believe that I'm worthy to be your mate as a human? You don't like humans. You killed humans. Even if you've changed your mind in the last century, surely you didn't change that much."

She says it in a rush, like she must get the words out now, and I'm left staring at her.

I don't need to ask her to clarify. I don't need any more information. I'm sure I can guess what stories are told about me.

Especially to the pretty human who's forced to visit me regularly.

I've never told her how I ended up here. I've never had to tell anyone what brought me this low. But I've hurt her, clearly, by not telling her. And it's time to rectify that.

If anyone in the world is owed the complete, unvarnished truth, it is Leana. And she deserves to make whatever decisions she will with it.

CHAPTER SEVENTEEN

LEANA

"You asked me what I saw in the mirror," he says, voice low and almost expressionless.

I nod. "You said fire."

"That's half of it."

I wait, not sure if I want to hear what will come next. I shouldn't have disturbed the past, maybe.

But I need to know. And he's apparently going to tell me.

"And the other half?" I ask softly, trying to let him know that I'm ready to listen.

"It was all shadow, but there was a shape. A human shape, and I knew that fire could never come from any dragon. It was too much, too bright—if it was dragon fire, it was like no dragon I'd ever seen."

"So there was a human. A magic user?" I ask. Like me? Someone else who can wield flames?

"That's what I thought. And I was determined. I told myself it was mostly curiosity. I know my reputation has likely drastically changed in the last century, but I used to largely be known as a researcher of sorts. Oh, people knew I was fierce, and no one doubted I'd kill for this kingdom, and I'd like to think I ruled relatively effectively alongside my brothers. But by and large I was a researcher. An eccentric, probably. As liable to go traveling to make trade agreements as to find some obscure magical artifact. So I convinced myself that I was just curious. That I wanted to understand the mirror, and needed to see it work to properly understand it. And to do that, I needed to force the moment in the mirror to come true. It was a charitable view of myself. But who turns down power when they're confronted by it? My brothers couldn't, and now my nephew is desperate for it. And I was no better."

"What did you do?" I ask, because I've never heard the story quite this way. I know where it has to lead; hundreds dead, including all his brothers but one.

How does a man start how he describes, commit the atrocities I know of, and end up here, today, being the man who he is? Something in the middle simply feels like it doesn't fit.

"I treated it like an experiment," he says. "Of course. Exactly as foolish, young me... anyways. I gathered every human magic user I could possibly find in the entire kingdom. Some came willingly. Others, I acquired them."

"You took them," I say bluntly.

"Folly of the dragon. We tend to view things as ours. And when one is already a ruler, with power over people..." His tail hits the wall. "Well. I did that. I gathered them all, testing them."

My stomach suddenly feels queasy at just the thought. "What does testing them mean?"

"Not what you're thinking, likely. I won't pretend it was the right choice to make, what I did. But I wasn't cruel. I demanded to see their powers. I wasn't kind about it. I was their king; I demanded their allegiance. But I didn't hurt them, at least not physically." He sighs. "But then my brothers learned what I had. And what I was trying to do. And as you've seen in our current situation, treasure, that damned mirror is essentially irresistible. Each of them wanted it, and they were willing to kill each other to get it. But first, they could agree they were willing to kill me to get it from me."

I'm beginning to imagine how this story might go, and it makes something inside me ache.

"None of the magic users I found could cause the flames I saw in the mirror. They could do many things, but not that. And then... most magic users aren't immune to dragon fire," he says. "And my brothers attacked, and I countered. If any of the humans survived, they were very few. Some must have, otherwise I don't know if magic ever would have flourished in this kingdom again."

But there are few of us at the castle with magic, and most of them can't do a quarter of what I can. Osir, bringing all the strong magic users to one place and painting a target on their backs, destroyed the magic for a century. It might never recover.

"I never got a good look at the devastation, truth be told. I made a decision. I hid the mirror, and then I came back, and even the briefest glimpse I got was enough. I knew my brothers weren't going to stop, so I killed them." He turns so I'm no longer leaning against him, so he can look me in the eye. "I say this because you need to understand. Deserve to understand what you're getting into with me. It's better and worse than the stories you've heard, I imagine. But you deserve the truth, so you can make up your mind."

I swallow, doing my best not to break his eye contact, although I have no idea what to say to that.

He didn't round up human magic users just to kill them. He's not single-handedly responsible for such a massacre, although he is culpable. And the ferocity in his eyes when he talks about killing his brothers, the grim determination...

Can I blame him for it, given what he's just told me? But I suppose that isn't his point; he wants me to know he's capable of that type of violence, whether or not I blame him for it.

I say the only thing I can think of. "I see now why you're insistent that the mirror remains hidden."

He's silent for a long moment, but then dips his head in a nod, breaking eye contact. "Yes, you can see the terrible ramifications of it. I wish I never uncovered it nearly every day." He doesn't move for a long moment. "Leana, treasure—I'm begging you to tell me what you're thinking."

"A whole generation of magic users lost," I breathe.

His tail shakes the cavern again. "Yes," he agrees, and I think that it's shame in his voice.

"The story is you rounded them up and killed them yourself. A fit of insanity, a refusal to let humans have magic. That you single-handedly and deliberately took that away from us."

"That was never my intention, but I suppose Braxil was the winner. Four brothers dead, me imprisoned finally; he gets to tell his story."

"How'd he imprison you? If your brothers were already dead..."

"Oh, he had plenty of dragons on his side. Enough to overwhelm me. And here we are." He jerks one of his chained legs. "Once these were on, it was done. I can't change my shape, can't use my strength. I'm helpless."

I take a deep, deep breath. The story is horrifying, but I've believed my whole life this man killed human magic users with deliberation. Is the tragedy more tolerable now that I've heard the story?

For me, I find that it is. And perhaps that would be shameful to all those who died. But I can't speak for them.

I deliberately lean back against him, letting my full weight press into his scales. "Thank you for telling me the truth."

He blows out a long breath, and his shoulder muscle relaxes under me. "I will always tell you the truth," he promises. "Even when it's not favorable to me. Even when it might make you leave me. I would be remiss if I didn't remind you that you could leave right now, Leana. All the wealth I hid is yours. You could run off, be safe, build a life for yourself, and never see me again."

Something in me goes a little soft at hearing that. Even though I have no intention of ever taking him up on that offer, the fact that he's so insistent on making it is touching.

"And what if I only want treasure that you give me?" I say, feeling bold. This man has promised me so many things, and I find myself believing him now. Me, a nobody, worth nothing, but I can't keep out his words, assuring me of my worth, my value to him, and it's made me bold. "You, yourself, from your own two hands?"

Because he will get out of here; I refuse to doubt it any longer. How can a man feel so much, think so much, and be confined down here?

He'll get out. He has to.

He's silent for a long moment, and I worry that perhaps I did overstep, that my boldness isn't appreciated. But he finally says, "I will give you more treasure than you could ever possibly wear. I'll give you a mountain of it, mate."

I close my eyes, pressing my face against his warm scales. "I don't want a mountain."

His tail flicks. "You're worth a mountain."

I've never had jewels or any fine things in my entire life. I don't need it. But I can tell it's important to him. "From your own two hands only," I remind him, lethargy creeping up my spine.

I'm exhausted. A lot has happened today, really.

"You underestimate me, treasure. A new piece every day for the rest of your life, delivered from my own two hands every morning. I'll await your approval, will live for nothing else."

The idea is ridiculous, but I play along. "I would never reject anything you give me."

"And when you do approve of it, it'll be my honor to put it on you, to watch your beauty give purpose and radiance to whatever piece I find you that day. It'll be a poor comparison to your beauty, of course. But I'll try my best, Leana."

"Stop it," I murmur. "I'm not that beautiful."

"You are the sun," he insists. "Too beautiful to look directly on, although I admit I find myself staring regardless."

He's ridiculous, but his words warm me. My fire means I never spent a cold night like so many in my position do, so I never knew I was cold inside. But there was evidently some part of me desperate for warmth, and his words are the only thing I've ever known to provide it.

It's ridiculous and too much and truly unnecessary, but I'd do anything to keep hearing his words.

"Osir?" I ask.

"Yes, treasure?"

"This is real, right?" I check. "What you're saying—you mean it?"

"That you're beautiful? I swear it, Leana, and—"

"No," I dare to interrupt. "I mean your promises."

"A new jewel every day? Of course. I'm a rich dragon, treasure."

"That you'll get out of here. That you really will give me jewels with your own two human hands, free from here."

I've let myself start believing him. I've let myself start dreaming of it. And I don't know what I'll do if I have to confront the likelihood that these dreams aren't possible.

He's silent for a long moment, making me squirm. But then he says, "Yes, treasure. I mean it. I swear to you—I'll make that happen." And he says it with such utter conviction that I can't help but believe it.

Chapter Eighteen

OSIR

My treasure sleeps against me once more, even though I was convinced not an hour ago she would flee and leave me behind forever.

I wouldn't have blamed her. While I know she was kind and even affectionate when she believed the horror stories spread about me, the truth is honestly not much better. I thought hearing it might be the thing that broke us.

It still might be, I remind myself forcibly. She might change her mind if she thinks it over long enough.

And I have to allow her. Even more, I have to enable her to do so. I have to make that easy for her to do.

I would be a poor mate to trap my treasure. But even more so, if I trap another human magic user for my own selfish ends, then I will have learned nothing. All of this would be worth nothing. I have not spent a century imprisoned to not have learned my damned lesson.

I will offer again to fund her freedom. I will offer every day, if that's what it takes. Leana will be free to choose me or not, but I will not imprison her here.

And to that same end, I cannot delay any longer. I cannot wait for an escape scenario that is entirely favorable to me. I must be free to give Leana freedom.

Either I will keep my promise and present my mate with new jewels every day—given to her by my own two human hands, as she insisted—or I will keep my promise to fund her escape. Either way, I will not be down here, entrapping her with her kind heart and pity for me.

I shouldn't sleep. I should consider the best path forward.

But if this is my last night to sleep with my mate, I won't waste it. I wrap around her the best I can and close my eyes, focusing on her soft breathing, letting her lull me to sleep.

***

I wake sometime later but refuse to open my eyes, feeling the barely there weight of Leana against my scales and basking in it.

If she leaves today, then I will accept it. I will enjoy every moment I have left in this hellhole, knowing it means she is free and living her life. And I will get through the nights by remembering this moment.

I can feel her stirring awake, and the selfish core of my soul wants to freeze time, to keep this moment forever.

But time doesn't work that way, not even for kings, so I wait for her to wake up entirely.

"Did you sleep?" she asks me, her voice rough, and it makes something warm build inside me, something entirely different from the dragon's fire.

"I did," I assure her. "Never better, treasure. Can I get you some food?"

Let me feed her one last time, at least. Another moment for me to carry in my soul if this is the last day we have together.

She pulls away from me, and I watch hungrily as she unfolds her still-naked limbs, food entirely forgotten in the face of her beauty.

I temporarily forget the dream of presenting her jewels every morning. Now I think of her waking up like this, stretching those tantalizing limbs in our bed.

Would she like waking up with my head between her thighs? Would that please my treasure? Because nothing on this earth, no gold or thrones or mystical artifact, would please me more.

She steps away from me, and I can't help how my eyes are drawn to her ass. I move to follow her hypnotically swaying hips, and the chain around my ankle drags against my skin, reminding me of where I am.

To my immediate disappointment, Leana finds her clothes and re-dresses. I watch as she hides her beautiful skin under that coarse cloth, and mentally push getting her nicer clothes higher on my list of things to worry about.

I tear my eyes away from her long enough to sort out food for the two of us, leaving the wine aside. As pleasant as reading and drinking together was yesterday, I need us both in full possession of our faculties today.

She comes over and takes her place sitting beside me, and I drop some bread and cheese into her lap. "Thank you," she says, and I feel the weight of it when she picks up my food and begins to eat.

She looks at me the whole time, too. She knows perfectly well what this means, for her to choose to continue to eat my food, even after last night.

"I have yet another favor to ask you," I tell her when we've both eaten a good portion of our meals.

She swallows the bite she's currently chewing and gives me her full attention. "Alright. What can I do?"

"I'm sending you back to the castle again."

She seems to go very still for a moment, but then nods. "Alright. What do you want me to say?"

"I want you to convince my damned nephew to come here. To bargain with me himself. Do you think you could do that?" I ask my question with genuine concern; I've not been impressed with her descriptions of my nephew, and will fully understand if she doesn't want to approach him again.

"Yes. I might need to imply that you indicated you'd give him the mirror if he came. But I can get him to come." She sounds confident as she says it, too, and never breaks eye-contact.

"That's fine. Tell him whatever you need to."

"What do you plan to do once he's here?" she asks me, and something inside me warms with the tone. My queen has found a deep reserve of force inside her, and talks to me like the equal she is.

Which is exactly why this is so necessary. "I plan to tell him I'll win his damn war, I'll secure his throne, and in exchange, he frees me and you, and lets us live our lives in peace."

The pronouncement is met with silence. "Why now?" she asks, half-strangled.

"Because I cannot abide being a dragon in chains anymore. Not when I could be a man at your side."

A small smile breaks across her face, and if I ever doubted I was making the right choice, the smile alone banishes such doubt.

If I do this for my nephew, I won't be a king. I will lose the castle and the crown. I won't be able to make my Leana a queen.

But I'll make sure she knows she is my queen every day, regardless. That will never change.

"I'll go now," she says, nodding her head. "With luck I can get him here today."

I want to leave it there. I want to wish her well, tell her I long for her return, and have that be the end of the conversation. But there is one more thing I feel duty bound to remind her of.

"Before you go," I tell her, "I need to know that you know how to find my hoard. Because if you choose not to come back to me—if you choose to wash your hands of this entire situation and leave me behind—I wouldn't blame you in the slightest. But I won't have you go in poverty, Leana. Please. My hoard is unaccessible, but there is a cache buried that I could direct you to. It would be plenty for you to build a new life with."

Leana moves fluidly to her feet, then walks towards me, eyes determinedly locked on mine. I don't dare move. I don't even breathe.

She puts her hand on the end of my snout and I think even my heart stops beating, waiting for her judgment.

Then she does the last thing I expect; she leans forward and presses a kiss to my snout.

"Silly dragon," she murmurs. "I'll be back, with the prince. We are getting you out of here, Osir. That's a promise."

I cannot describe the feeling coursing through me to hear her say it. My heart, as if to make up for its earlier refusal to beat, beats double-time now. But I have to be sure.

"Even so," I insist. "The wealth is yours and I need you to know. Please."

She steps back and every inch of me wants to protest, but the smile she gives me is almost worth the price of the distance. "Alright," she agrees. "But I meant what I said, Osir. I'll only take treasure from your own two hands."

If that's what she wants, then she shall have it. More treasure than even the greediest dragon would ever know what to do with. Enough riches to fill entire rooms.

I just have to get out of here first.

Chapter Nineteen

Leana

W hen I emerge from the cave, I'm surprised to realize it's night.

I woke up an hour or so ago, fully convinced it was morning. I suppose the darkness of being so far under the earth causes us to lose time.

Thankfully, dawn is breaking by the time I make it to the castle. Arriving unexpectedly at a castle preparing for war in the middle of the night seems like a poor choice.

The sun has barely broken the horizon, but the castle is still a buzz of activity. I frown. While servants of course always get an early start on the day, there are simply too many people moving about for this to be normal.

"I'm here to see the prince," I tell the gate guard. "I've been sent on an errand for him and am just returning. He'll want to see me."

"He doesn't have time to see the likes of you," he grumbles, barely looking at me. He has prominent bags under his eyes, and his attention is constantly diverted by the bustling chaos around us.

"He personally sent me out to obtain materials for the war. I'm returning." I hope he takes with said materials as implied. If possible, I would like to avoid lying. Whatever they choose to believe about what I say is, of course, an entirely different matter.

"Listen to me. The king doesn't have time for the likes of you."

I blink. "I'm here for the prince."

"Ain't no prince anymore."

It feels like all the air is sucked out of the room. "The king is dead?" I manage to ask.

"Yesterday. Where you been that you didn't hear it?"

Deep underground, but I don't say it.

I lift my chin and narrow my eyes, trying to project confidence. It feels ridiculous, but then I think about how I feel when Osir speaks to me. If I can pretend to be half the person he seems to think I am, then this will be easy.

"I have a way to win this war," I tell him. "That's what I was sent for. The king will want to see me."

***

It takes until nearly midday before I am finally shown into the same room where Noctere first assigned me the task of finding that wretched mirror.

I'm left alone there, and only reasonably confident that Noctere will actually arrive.

Noctere. The king. I've never interacted with King Braxil personally, and no one has seen him at all in so long. But even so, the world feels different now.

I knew Noctere as a child. I knew a prince who scorned his lessons and rather wrestle in the mud than practice diplomacy. I knew a boy whose temper tantrums almost killed people and robbed us both of mothers. And as of now, that boy is somehow in charge of a kingdom.

A kingdom shortly to be at war, no less. I hope he's smart enough to be grateful for what Osir is offering. Surely Noctere is overwhelmed and not ready to confront a war on his own.

Noctere comes storming into the room, throwing the door open and causing me to jump. His heavy boots make noise even through the rugs covering the floor, and I wither under the intensity of his eyes. This man is close to losing his control.

Well, he did just lose his father.

"Your highness," I say, barely remembering to address him with his title. Even a few days with Osir have altered me so much. "Or I suppose it's your majesty now."

He doesn't sit, just pacing near the head of the table. "So, you heard."

"I just heard this morning, your majesty. I'm sorry for your loss."

"Yes well..." He sighs, and stops moving. "Two parents in one day. It's been..." He shakes his head. "It doesn't matter. It's irrelevant to why you're here."

It doesn't feel irrelevant to me, though. "Your mother?" I ask quickly. "You know where she is? Your majesty?" I belatedly remember to tack on.

"Of course I know where my mother was," he scoffs, and resumes his pacing.

"Was?"

"How else did you think my father died? He wasn't that old, Leana. And it's almost impossible to kill a dragon. Much easier to just let their mate die."

"What?" I ask, trying to understand what he means while I feel like some sort of heavy weight is settling in my stomach.

He stops moving again and turns to face me. "I forget how ignorant you humans can be," he mutters, and I'd feel offended, but he's talking.

And why shouldn't he? I doubt he's been able to talk about anything but succession and the war in days. As far away as our childhood is, I might still be the only person he can be foolish and honest with.

"Dragons don't survive the loss of a mate," he says, pacing again. "They never have in recorded history, as far as I know."

My heart catches in my throat. Osir—I never knew I had to be worried for more than just myself, if I got sent off to war.

He didn't tell me. He didn't tell me on purpose, I realize with a sharp sinking feeling. He had ample opportunity to say something, but he chose not to. He doesn't want me to worry, I know. He doesn't want me to think of him, trapped in that hell, dying alone.

Well, I can hardly get it out of my mind now.

"But I thought dragons could live thousands of years," I protest, trying to return to the conversation at hand.

He waves a hand as if dismissing my claim, not turning fully towards me. "Yes, yes. If the mate accepts the bond, then both parties can tie their life-force together forevermore. Neither will die without the other, and they're far more likely to live a dragon's lifespan, even if one party had a measly human life when they mated." I bristle at the dismissal, but I don't contradict him, biting my tongue.

Osir might want to protect me from worry, but I fully intend to return to him shortly, and live a life together, if he'll still have me even once he's free. And I'll need to know these things.

"It's an active thing," he continues to explain after a moment, as if my continued silence is the permission he needs to keep talking. "Dragons mate for life, and it's irreversible.

Hence why my father couldn't let my mother go even after she had the gall to abandon him. But if one mate is a human, they can walk away. They can break the bond on their end."

So she had sickened and finally died, I conclude, without him needing to say. She had not benefited from King Braxil's lifespan, and he had suffered hers.

I wonder if his mother had known what he just told me. I wonder if she regretted not having Braxil's life in the end. Maybe she was pleased to know she was taking the husband she never much liked down with her, at the end.

Then I feel guilty for the thought. Her death was not an elaborate revenge plan. She was merely a woman who was sick, and likely died in terrible pain.

Some small part of me—the kindest part—can hope my mother was able to comfort her during this long illness.

"You knew where she was?" I ask softly.

He stops and turns fully to me. "Your mother didn't ask about you," he says, and I can hear the jeer in the words.

He needs someone to lash out at, I distantly realize, and I am convenient and entirely permissible for him to target, because I can never lash back. Knowing this doesn't stop the anger bubbling in my gut, a pot almost boiling over. My fire seems to rise, pushing it to boil even faster.

But I doubt his mother was happy to see him, either. His very dragon-ness terrified her enough that she ran off in the night, taking my mother with her and leaving both of us behind.

I don't ask about his visit to his mother. I can guess how it went. And as bitter and unfair as it is, that calms some of my anger.

The man lost two parents in one day, was thrust upon a throne that it is clear as day he feels unprepared for, and has a looming war to prepare for. But I have good news to bring him, if I can make him listen to it.

"I have something for you," I tell him.

"The mirror. Where is it?"

"He won't give up the mirror. Not to me, at least," I say hastily, watching the rage like fire cloud his eyes. "He wants to meet with you."

"Do I look like I have the time to meet with mad old kings?"

"The man is your uncle," I try. "He's told me his offer to help is genuine. As long as he meets you."

"And I suppose you believed him?"

"You sent me to convince him. This is what I have."

"It's not enough!" he bursts, turning to face me fully, walking closer with rapid, heavy steps. I sink back in my chair, but there's nowhere to go. "I sent you to end this war, Leana. I sent you to take care of this one thing. And you're merely adding more complications to my plate."

I want to tell him I'm not a soldier, an advisor, or a courtier. I am not meant to do this type of work, and I am not meant to uncomplicate a war. I am merely a servant who sweeps floors and brings meals to a prisoner, and yet I challenge anyone to have convinced Osir to help the kingdom like I did. I want to say it.

I keep my mouth shut. It won't help.

"This is the best solution I have to offer, your majesty," I say, trying to keep my eyes down and demure, despite the threat looming over me. "I'm sorry it's not what you wanted. But I do believe he's genuine in his offer to help."

He lets out an inhuman growl, and for the first time I find myself truly afraid of Noctere. Not of the power he has, but of him physically. His fire might not be able to hurt me, but he could rip me apart with barely a thought.

I've always known he could. But for the first time, I genuinely fear that he might.

"You're a fool to believe him," he snarls. "And I don't have time to chase his false promises. War will be here any day now. The news of my father's death won't be kept quiet, and those princes of Ashar will think we're ripe for the picking. And without that stupid mirror—" He trails off for a long moment. "We don't have it. They won't get it. We need to turn them back at the border."

I risk looking up, and find his eyes gleaming as he looks at me. "I did what you asked," I croak. "I did—"

"You failed," he interrupts, voice as sharp as his eyes. "You let me down, Leana. But maybe you'll do better when you understand that your life is actually on the line. Every piece has their use, and we'll find one for you."

My hands start shaking as I try to grip the table. Noctere just told me it's not just my own life on the line, although of course he doesn't know it.

"I did what you asked," I say again, but it sounds pathetic even to my own ears.

"And you'll continue to do so," he says, voice savage with power. "The least you owe your sovereign. Guards!" he snaps, voice raised, and I push myself to my feet as the door behind us swings open.

"Leana is due at the front. See she gets there," he says, turning away to dismiss me.

"You don't get to treat me like this!" I shout at him, desperation making my voice rough. I'm proud of myself for saying it, for shouting at him. I can almost hear Osir in the back of my mind, grumbling his approval, telling me I'm worth arguing for.

He turns back to me, and I see cold death promised in his eyes, but I think I also see the desperation he's so determined to hide under it. "I am king, I can do whatever I need for this kingdom," he snarls.

"I have done everything you've ever asked! You do not get to send me to die to prove a point."

Clawed fingers dig into my arms. "Show the king the proper respect he deserves, or you'll start your first day at the front with a whipping."

I jerk my arm away from him, but his grip doesn't budge. He only tightens his fingers, and I feel claws digging into my flesh, a violent warning of things to come.

Noctere just looks lost, like the little boy I remember him being. "You still have the potential to be immensely useful to the kingdom. With your magic, we could genuinely stand a chance. You're the strongest human magic user we have—we'll have use for you," he says, trying to justify this. Desperation clouds his eyes, as if he can just keep talking, maybe I'll understand. I refuse to blink, staring him down. "Leana, when you do this for me—when you come back—you'll be rewarded. You'll be a crucial part of our army. You'll have titles, lands, wealth—whatever you want."

I don't want his titles and lands. I don't want a consolation prize. I don't want to let him justify sending me to die. I just stare him down.

His pleading eyes don't drop mine for a long minute, but he at last looks away. He turns to leave, and the dragon yanks on my arm again. "Let's go."

I light my entire body on fire. I can't help it; it churns inside me, somewhere deep down, stoked by my fear and something that feels frighteningly close to hatred, and the only relief is to release my hold on the flames and let them bubble up to my skin.

The dragon lets go, and I move out of his reach, setting my face into what I hope is an expression that conveys he doesn't want to mess with me.

"Bitch," he snarls. "You want to play with fire? Let a dragon show you fire."

"No—" Noctere calls, turning back to the proceedings, but he's too late. The guard has already opened his mouth, exhaling a great gust of fire with a roar, and I welcome it.

It joins my flames, mingling with the brighter fire on my body, until I am surrounded by a mist of swirling, luminous flames.

I turn away from the dragon who just tried to kill me. If he tries again, I'll welcome it.

I find Noctere's eyes across the room, and his eyes can't hope to hide his fear now. "You should have known better," I tell him. "But perhaps she was right to be afraid of you."

Bringing his mother into the conversation is an absolutely paralyzing blow for him, and we both stand there frozen for a minute.

Metal clanks against my wrist, and I look down to see it. The second guard apparently came prepared to drag me away, willingly or unwillingly. The shackle bites into my skin, and it's clear Noctere had them ready to bring me to the front lines bound and trussed like a prisoner if necessary.

I want to shout at him some more. I want to tell the scared little boy in his eyes that he is everything his mother feared, that his father was a terrible king, that he should have trusted me.

I don't. He won't listen, anyway.

"Don't follow me," I say, and I burn the cuff away to nothing, leaving it a melted pile of sludge on the floor, and back out of the room.

Perhaps Noctere thought his word as king and the chains would be enough to make me do his bidding. Perhaps any other guards he had at the ready are rightfully frightened of the woman blazing like a star in the daytime. Either way, no one stops me as I leave the castle.

Chapter Twenty

OSIR

The clanging of the gate and the footsteps I'd recognize anywhere in the world put a stop to my brooding thoughts.

Then the entire cavern lights up. At first it's just a gentle glow, like perhaps more torches were lit by some unseen servant without me noticing. But as the footsteps get nearer, it gets brighter, until I have to squint my eyes.

It's like being back outside under the sun, a sensation I've nearly forgotten the intensity of after a century.

When Leana finally enters the cavern, the light is so bright I physically cannot look at her. I chance a peek regardless—I am incapable of resisting my treasure—and see the swirling vortex of fire before I'm forced to look away.

Her body is just a shadow among all that fire, and I now know for certain what I've suspected for some time.

All those poor human magic users I got killed were for nothing, because the true secret of power in this kingdom would not be born for nearly another century.

And here she stands before me, too radiant for my unworthy eyes. A human magic user, a servant, my greatest treasure and our future queen.

Something in me purrs in satisfaction. I always knew my treasure was special, but this just proves it. I wonder if she knows what power she holds. I wonder when this entire kingdom will realize it.

"You are a goddess in flames," I proclaim, meaning every word. I will worship her gladly.

"I'm here to free you," she says, her voice muffled by the crackling flames.

"What?" Perhaps I misheard her, because that was not the plan. "What of my nephew?"

"Didn't want to come. Tried to send me to die in war. Which I'm now given to understand would have more serious consequences than I thought," she concludes, a sharp preciseness to her words telling me she's angry with me.

"There could be no more serious consequence for the world than you not being in it," I proclaim honestly. Me dying with her is an afterthought, and one she should never have to worry about.

"You should have told me my death would kill you."

I didn't want her to know. I didn't want my kind-hearted mate to fear for me. I intended to keep this from her until I could ensure that her lifespan was just as tied to mine, until I could give her centuries, perhaps millennia.

"Listen to me," I say, forcing myself to look into the flames. "It would be an honor to die with you, treasure. And a blessing, because I'll not live in a world without you." The very thought of doing so is abominable. But also not what I should focus on right now. "Did he hurt you?"

If my nephew laid so much as a hand on her, then I will take back all my plans. I will show him that it is more than possible to kill a dragon, and I am an expert at it. I will burn everything he cares for to the ground.

She laughs. It sounds almost broken, fragile, and my body aches, but I don't know how to fix it. "Do I look like they could hurt me right now?"

Yes, because she is a human, and their bodies are fragile. Yes, because all it takes is a claw, teeth, the crushing weight of a fully transformed dragon. But I take her point.

She seemingly doesn't need an answer from me, walking further into the cavern with determined steps. She draws close enough that I'm once more forced to close my eyes, unable to stand up to her brightness.

"I think I can melt your cuffs," she says. "Would you allow me to try?"

Could she? Could she break them when I tried for a century and they never so much as budged?

I banish the thought. She is my mate, and she is the one I saw in the mirror. Of course she can.

"The front ones," I tell her. "They're the more heavily enchanted ones. If you can get those ones, I think I can transform."

The heat only increases as she steps closer. I obediently lower my chained limbs to her reach, and she places her flaming hands right on the metal.

The heat of it licks at my skin. After a moment, the prickling sensation turns to pain. I've never felt pain from fire before, but I can bear it.

The metal melts away under her touch, like liquid ore from the smith, like it hasn't been an enchanted, unbreakable cuff for the last century.

I flex in my new freedom, staring at the limb with disbelief as the last tendrils of her fire lick around it. "I—you are a marvel, my treasure, my beautiful, perfect treasure," I murmur, and I hope she can hear the awe.

I look up, ready to continue extolling her virtues, but then I realize I can make out her face clearer. I can look upon her again, and while I, of course, always appreciate seeing my treasure, this must mean her fire is dying down, banked back to a more typical level.

She notices when I do and closes her eyes, tightening her muscles, like she's trying to summon more flames. I've never seen her try even half as hard to summon flames, but her increased effort doesn't change anything.

I try to remove her need to summon more, trying to bring forth my own magic. If I can just transform, I can slip these cuffs and give her everything I promised her. Perhaps with one cuff gone, the enchantment holding me will be weakened and I will overcome it—

I'm held fast.

"Treasure?" I ask, because now it looks like her attempts to summon more are physically paining her.

She opens her eyes. "I absorbed his fire," she says quickly. "I didn't become like that until I absorbed it. That's the solution. I need your fire."

"Who? My nephew?" I demand. Who dared try to attack my mate? It hardly matters that it clearly didn't work.

"Who? No. Some soldier. I need you to focus, Osir," she says. "I need you to hit me with a blast of fire."

"I will not attack my mate." The thought makes me physically ill.

"It can't hurt me."

Maybe not, but mates don't attack each other. I'm meant to treasure her, love her, adore her. How can I do that if I'd commit violence towards her?

"You have to do this. I'm asking you. Please, Osir. Because if you don't—then we can't be free together. You can't protect me from the war. And you can't give me the jewels you promised me."

"That is not fair," I grumble, but I already know she is going to win. She could ask anything of me, I imagine. "Hold still. You're absolutely sure it doesn't hurt?"

"It can't hurt me. It'll just make me stronger."

If she is wrong about this—if I am wrong, if I risk her health and safety—then I will never forgive myself. But I want the future she promises more than I've ever wanted anything. It ignites an ache deep inside me, stirring my own fire, until at last I close my eyes, unable to watch, and give my mate everything I have.

I open my eyes, only to immediately close them. She's glowing so brightly it's impossible to see anything else. She is the sun in human form.

"Hold still," she says, stepping closer to me, bringing the burning heat as she does. She finds my other cuff and places her hand on it, and I think we both hold our breath while we wait to see what happens.

Just when the pain begins to really irritate me, the cuff melts. Some of the metal disappears, turning into vapor upon contact with Leana's skin, and the rest falls to the ground, liquid and useless.

I am free. After a century, I am free.

CHAPTER TWENTY-ONE

OSIR

I don't waste a second. I find that thread inside me, the one I can tug to turn back to a human form. What once was so easy to do feels foreign now, but I don't let that stop me. I have my treasure here, after all, and after all these years, I am more than ready to hold her.

The disorientation from the change almost sends me to my knees, and then I look at my still flaming mate and really do go to my knees, my naked, human shins scraping on the stones.

Here she is, bracketed by flames, a vision so beautiful I almost don't believe it's real. "Treasure," I groan, looking up at her in awe.

My voice doesn't echo as it did before, the rumble of a too-large diaphragm gone. This is a voice meant for whispering sweet nothings in her ear, for whispering dirty promises between her thighs.

I am, at last, exactly who I was meant to be for her.

That realization makes something snap into place within me, something self-satisfied, like a purring animal. I am here. I am hers.

She must not realize that I am basking in euphoria, because she runs the last few steps to me, flames flickering out against her skin, seemingly forgotten. "Osir!" she calls, falling to her knees before me, reaching out, and the first touch of her hands on my bare chest makes me want to groan.

I want to touch her back more than I want to breathe, so I move, carefully taking her hands from my chest and clasping both of them in my own. Her hands are so small against mine, and I can't resist the urge to bring them to my lips, kissing over calluses and knuckles and fingertips.

"You are perfect," I tell her, voice slightly muffled as I compulsively press kisses to her skin. "You are—"

I don't get to finish my statement, because she wrenches her hands from mine, and before I can voice my objection, she throws them around my neck, hugging me close and burying her face in my shoulder.

I don't hesitate to wrap her in my arms. "My beautiful treasure, you saved me," I murmur, rubbing along her back.

She seems overwrought, but I'd like to believe that my presence is comforting.

I'd hold her here forever, but my promises—to both her and myself—are nagging at the back of my mind. I look up from her dark hair, glancing around the cavern that was my cell for so long. I'm ashamed to still have her here. It's time to go, and I'll never let her be trapped underground again.

"Leana," I sigh her name into her hair. "My treasure, you need to make a choice."

Her fingers dig into my back, like she won't release me, and I savor the press of skin against skin, but I nudge her gently, needing her attention.

"What choice?" she asks after a moment.

"You came back to me. You freed me. Can I assume—is it presumptuous to think—would you deign to spend your life with me, treasure?"

"Is that the question?" she demands, pulling back, much to my displeasure. I think I see flames in her eyes when she stares at me. "You don't trust me to stay?"

"I trust you with everything," I deny. "I simply know you deserve better."

"Me? You're free, Osir. You could be a king again. Your brother is dead, this kingdom is in turmoil. I imagine it's ripe for the picking. You could be king again by tomorrow and I'll still just be a servant. Are you sure you want me?"

"If I am a king tomorrow, you will be a queen. If you are a servant tomorrow, then I shall learn to work beside you," I proclaim, then swallow. I move my hands from her back to cup her face. "If you will do me the honor of staying with me, then I have a choice to give you."

She leans into my hand, eyes slipping partially closed, and I realize that I am not the only one here who has longed for the loving touch of a mate. This sensation coursing through me feels almost like power, although it's not any type of power I've ever felt before.

It's intoxicating, and I stroke my thumb over her cheekbone.

"Tell me, then," she murmurs.

"I can have us gone from this kingdom within the hour," I tell her. "We can forget it all and start over again. We will live in luxury, and I will endeavor everyday to make sure you want for nothing." I don't know anything about what has happened in neighboring kingdoms in the last century, but I do know that wealth opens many doors. I can buy a manor and safety for us easily enough.

"Or?"

"Or I can continue with what we originally planned. I can go to my nephew and make us a place in this kingdom. Although I'll admit, with my brother dead and my nephew very clearly deserving of a sound thrashing—perhaps I will take a, hm, more active role in the future of this kingdom. If you'll allow it."

Perhaps I'll kill him. I don't say it out loud, but I can't stop considering it.

She huffs. "It's not my place to allow you that."

"It is your place and your place alone. I will not do it if you don't wish for it. But in truth, I'd see you as a queen, Leana. A beautiful, kind, fire-wreathed queen."

She stares at me, her dark eyes pools I would happily drown in. I hold my breath, waiting for her decision.

"I want to stay here," she finally pronounces. "I don't know about being queen, but I think this kingdom needs help. Your help, if you're willing to give it."

I smile at her. "Whatever my queen commands. We should go—but there's one thing to do first."

"Oh?" she asks, looking around the cave. "What?"

I promised myself when I first confessed what she was to me that I would not push any further until I was free. But I promised myself that I would present jewels and riches at the earliest opportunity.

Dragons will happily, ecstatically, shower their mate in gold every day for centuries, but it is that first piece that is the most meaningful. The acceptance of that first piece represents acceptance of the bond, and I ache to have more than words between us.

Of course, there's no jewelry in this cave.

There is a pile of re-solidifying iron on the ground, and I seriously study it for a moment. With dragon fire and a little effort, I'm sure I could shape a bracelet of some sort from it.

But it would be ugly, and that frankly is the least of my concerns.

Whatever form it takes, she and I would still know that it's a shackle, and you simply don't put a shackle on a queen.

Finalizing our bond will have to wait. I owe her better than this.

But she's still waiting for an answer, and I know one thing I would very much like to have, something we don't need to wait for. "May I have a kiss?" I ask.

She doesn't even hesitate, nodding against my palm, so I lean in, gently guiding her face to meet mine.

Our lips feel like fire, a building, raging inferno that could consume the entire world. Her kiss is clumsy, and I fear I'm a century out of practice and so in awe of her that I'm overwhelmed. It doesn't matter; when she sighs into my mouth, I think I could conquer the world to lay it at her feet.

My mate. My beautiful, perfect treasure, who I have watched and longed for for years. And she's here. Her face and her hip in my hand, her lips under mine.

Perhaps I'm dreaming, but then she grabs my neck, holding me in place like she's worried I'd ever actually move. And I could never imagine the feeling of her fingers on my skin. It's too perfect, too beyond my imagination.

The fire burns between us, building and building, but I force myself to stifle it. I won't bed my mate in this damn cell.

Neither of us should be trapped here any longer.

She seems to be thinking similar thoughts, because she pulls back, moving her hand from my neck to my face, stroking along my jaw. "You're free," she whispers, eyes locked on mine.

It's all I can do not to kiss her again. "We're free," I correct. I remind myself that I was once a king and I aim to be again. That I was clever, and strong, and decisive, and feared. And, knowing all these things, I should have the strength to stand and separate from my treasure for a moment.

There're jewels aplenty out of this cave, I remind myself, and that thought encourages me to stand. The future she deserves is waiting for us.

I stand and offer a hand to help her up, but she doesn't take it, gaping at me.

I look down at my naked body. It looks much the same as I remember. "Do you like it?" I ask her, genuinely curious.

If she doesn't like it...

She liked you as a dragon. Surely this will not be what chases her away, I remind myself forcefully, and with that little reassurance, I make myself stand and let her look her fill.

She's flushed when she accepts my hand, letting me pull her to her feet. Then, because I cannot possibly hope to resist her for even a moment, I pull her against my naked body.

Her hands land on my chest, and I dearly wish to let her touch me to her heart's content. But that must wait.

"It'll be difficult to climb out of here naked," she murmurs.

"We're not climbing."

"No?" she asks, and she strokes a finger along my skin, seemingly absent-mindedly. "Do you plan to stay here forever, then?"

"I plan to fly, my treasure. I swear on my life I won't let you fall."

"Fly?" she squeaks, but I've already forced myself to let her go so I can transform.

Pulling the thread to turn back to a dragon is easier than turning into a human, and I'm once more looking at the cavern from the vantage point I'm used to.

I hold out a large, scaled and clawed hand to my mate. "I swear I won't hurt you," I promise her, waiting for her to decide if she can do this.

She doesn't hesitate, carefully climbing past my claws and into my waiting grasp. I'm holding the most precious cargo, and I won't forget it.

As I've wanted to do for a century, I beat my wings and take off towards the world above.

Chapter Twenty-Two

LEANA

My stomach rolls, the world spinning around me as we rapidly soar out of the cave. I force my eyes closed, unable to process the quick ascent. It helps with the nausea, but only a little.

I realize very quickly that humans are simply meant to stay on the ground.

Then the air gets fresher, warmer. The scent of dank stone is replaced with fresh dirt. Osir's wings miss a beat.

He hasn't seen the sun in a century.

I want to say something. To touch him. To promise we can spend every day outside under the sun from now on. To promise we never have to go into that cave again.

He doesn't stop, though. He keeps flying, and I probably should have asked him where he intended to go before I let him pick me up like this.

"I smell smoke," he pronounces. The wind almost drowns out his voice, but nothing can quite erase that deep, rumbling noise.

"Smoke?" I ask, hoping he'll be able to hear me over the wind.

"Smoke," he confirms, and then there's a great swooping feeling. I open one eye to check, and we're flying higher, higher, the ground peeling away as if pulled out from under me.

Then he stops, flapping his wings to stay suspended in midair, and I close my eyes again. I'm sure the view of the kingdom is enchanting, but if I were meant to see it this way, I would have been born with wings.

"Dragon fire," he growls. The growl has enough force that it shakes me, and I risk opening my eyes to try to see what he does.

I can't, of course, because I never should have expected to have the sight of a dragon, and firmly close my eyes again.

"That is my village, in my kingdom, that has been attacked by a dragon."

I wish he'd land to have this conversation. The swooping in my stomach hasn't calmed at all.

"Noctere thought they'd attack as soon as they heard about your brother's death," I manage to tell him.

"So he's not entirely stupid, then. War has begun."

Perhaps Noctere was right. Perhaps I would be more useful there, especially now that we've all seen what I can do with dragon fire—

"What are you going to do?" I ask.

"I'm bringing you to safety," he responds immediately. "You're not going to war today, Leana." He pauses for a moment. "But I daresay I am."

And, without letting me react, he swoops lower, and I fight to not be sick.

***

At long last, the wind stops moving around us, and everything stops shaking. I peel one eye open.

Solid ground.

He sets me down like I'm made of glass, and by the time I can stand without feeling dizzy, he's transformed into a man once more.

He's a very stunning man, and I recognize that this isn't the time to focus on that, but I can't help myself. I know that a century means nothing in dragon aging, but it's startling to see someone who spent a century imprisoned looking so relatively young. If he was human, I wouldn't guess he's over forty. His hair hangs almost to his shoulders, a deep brown that has red woven into it when the sun hits it right. Red, like his scales, which creep up the sides of his bare shoulders and neck.

I ignore his nakedness—now is not the time to consider it, I remind myself, although I like to imagine that time might be coming soon—and fall into his waiting arms.

I bury my face in his bare chest, letting his touch warm me to my core, letting his arms around me prove that this is real.

"I'll be back," he says, kissing the top of my head. "I'm going to end this. If those princes of Ashar think they've found a nation in turmoil with a weak young king, then I will quickly correct that notion. In the meantime, stay here, please."

"Where is here?" I ask, not willing to pull away from him even long enough to look around.

"Our hoard," he says simply, stroking a hand down my back. "If no one found it in a century, then it's as safe as any place I could bring you. Trust me, they looked. If they didn't find it, then those Ashar princes won't."

"You'll be safe?" I ask, still refusing to let go.

"I am a dragon, treasure. And I refuse to be separated from you for long. I'll be back, safe, and ready to begin our life together."

That sounds wonderful, really.

He cups my face in his large hand, tilting it up so I'm looking at him. I want to drown in his eyes, such a light brown they might truly be gold. I want to study every plane, every line.

He leans down to kiss me senseless, and that is good, too. I learn the inside of his mouth, his lips, his tongue, soak in his taste and scent.

He pulls back, kissing my nose, then my forehead, and I close my eyes again, sinking into this moment with him.

"This is your hoard too now," he murmurs. "Go pick out every piece that you like. They're yours, and I'd be honored to present them to you as soon as I return."

I lean up to kiss him again, and he lets me, biting gently at my lower lip before pulling away. I open my eyes—to complain, to draw him back, just to watch his beauty—but he's already stepping away mid-transformation.

The change happens quickly, a blur of motion my eyes can't possibly hope to understand. My mind simply doesn't accept that a very reasonably sized man was just in the spot now occupied by a creature so big he makes this ledge look precariously small.

"Be safe," I say. What else does one say to their mate when they're headed to war?

He lowers his head and gently nudges against me. "I'll return soon," he promises, and then he takes off into the sky,

leaving me there outside this cave to watch until he disappears.

CHAPTER TWENTY-THREE

OSIR

If I didn't smell that damned smoke, I would have happily led my mate into that cave, presented her with her weight in jewelry, and fucked her until our bond took. It would have been the happiest day of my life.

But Leana says she wants to save this kingdom, so save it I shall. They say waiting makes things sweeter, although I think I've waited long enough for my mate by now.

At least she's safe. If Braxil never found my hoard, then I highly doubt anyone else will.

Hidden in the rocky crags of a cliff, the ledge is visible from the ground, but the cave mouth is not. Only the most determined soul would make the climb up here, and they'd risk falling with every step.

A dragon could fly up here, but the rocks are tight and difficult to navigate. They'd risk tearing a wing if they're not careful.

Leana is as safe as I can make her. And now I have a kingdom to save on her behalf.

My first instinct is to go to where that village burned. But if the Ashar soldiers already burned it, then they will be long gone.

No, there's a much more simple and elegant solution than flying until I spot something. A solution that will make my position in this war very clear.

I turn and head to the castle.

***

I land right in the center courtyard of my former castle, sending people scrambling to get out of my way. "Nephew!" I snarl. "Come out and face me, nephew!"

I take a quick look around while I'm making such a scene, looking for any dragons I might know from before my imprisonment. Anyone who might have the brains to tell my young and clearly foolish nephew that it would be a poor idea to fuck with me.

I see two. The first is Ganius, who must be nearing a millennium and a half in age now, and his human form looks weathered to prove it. The second is Lorcate, if I'm not mistaken. She was barely twenty when I last saw her, still learning her trade at her father's side, but she is all grown up now. At twenty, I considered her clever, reasonable, and formidable. I hope that a century has not changed that about her.

Osir, some of them whisper in the crowd. *It's him.*

Then, I finally hear them saying what I want to hear. Get the king.

"Yes, get him," I snarl, hoping that the fierce and unexpected threat will get his attention fast. No ruler in their right mind would want to leave me unattended in their courtyard. "Tell him his uncle has come."

Some people scramble out of the crowd, so I'm left to periodically snap to keep everyone at arm's reach.

Finally, my nephew emerges. He doesn't look much like his father, but there's something about the conceited, stubborn set to his mouth that gives it away.

The crown on his head is also a strong hint.

"Osir," he says, stopping just out of reach of my claws.

"Nephew. I have words for you. Would you like them here or in private?"

"How did you escape?"

I exhale, pushing a little smoke out through my nostrils. "Would you have words here or in private? Pick."

He bites his lip, and I want to roll my eyes. A king must be decisive, or at least keep indecisive moments private.

"Do you intend to do harm here?" he asks.

"Not unless provoked."

He nods, seemingly considering it, and I take his lapse in focus to make a point. Quick as a flash, I move my arm, grabbing him in one clawed hand, far less careful with my claws than I am when I'm with Leana.

There are screams as I pick him up and drag him closer, but I only focus on the look of terror on his face. In a moment, my untested nephew will pull his brain out of his ass and remember that he is a dragon with the power to transform into a clawed, fire-breathing beast, so I have to make my point quickly.

"I intend to do no harm," I snarl. "But I intend to never be locked up again. I have too many things to live for. So if harm is done to me, understand this: I will strike first and I will strike harder."

I drop him, none too gently, watching him bounce off the ground. He stands soon enough, seemingly no worse for wear physically, although he's rumpled and that stupid crown has fallen off his head, so I consider this a victory.

"F-follow me," he says, his voice shaking, and I find that string inside me once more, unweaving the dragon form and following him as a man.

The crowd parts around us, perhaps eager not to get in the middle of our squabble. But Ganius steps forward, offering me the cloak from his own back.

Right, nakedness. A strange thing to remember to be concerned about now.

There's no time to speak with him, to find out everything he has to say about the last century. What must he think of me? What did my brother say about me? Did he believe it?

A problem for later, I suppose, as I fasten the cloak and follow my nephew.

He leads me to a meeting room and I take the seat at the head of the table. Let us continue this how we mean to go on.

He glowers for a second, but as I suspected, he's hopelessly out of his depth and has no idea how to strike back at me. In truth, if he hadn't threatened Leana, I might take pity on him.

But he threatened Leana, so I'm still undecided on if he gets to live.

"How did you get free?" he demands again.

"How do you think?" Honestly. I'm genuinely worried about his intelligence.

Unexpectedly, he lunges forward. He stops himself quickly—the boy has some sense—but his eyes are wild. "Did you hurt her?"

A snarl rips out of my throat. I can't help it; I don't think he could have insulted me worse if he tried. Me, hurt Leana? I will die first.

"Leana is safe, and happy, and has asked me to help you," I snap. "She freed me."

"Freed you? How?" His aggressive posture melts away in confusion, and I grind my teeth.

Perhaps he's more pathetic than threatening. Of course, that is ultimately Leana's decision. But for now, I see the lost, confused boy sitting across the table from me.

"She's powerful. More powerful than any human magic user I've ever known."

"But why would she do that?"

So many answers. Because she's my mate? Because she asked me to save this kingdom? Because I promised her treasure and luxury? Because a fully turned dragon makes a particularly poor lover?

"Perhaps you will understand someday, when you find your mate."

"She's your mate?" he demands, incredulous.

I bristle at that. "Do you doubt my mate?"

He freezes, very much aware of the thin ice he has trod on here. A dragon's mate is both their greatest strength and their greatest weakness, and it would be a poor decision to cross me about mine.

"All this time..." he murmurs, then his face darkens. "I trusted her!"

He couldn't sound more like the child throwing temper tantrums from Leana's story if he tried. I think I might genuinely pity him.

"And I daresay she trusted you, and you paid her back by threatening to kill her and me by sending her to war." Not that Leana knew of my own death until today. But dragon-to-dragon, I need Noctere to understand what he did.

"War is coming. I can't stop it. I need every asset I can get. If I can't have that mirror, then Leana's magic will do."

Over my dead body will I allow Noctere to look into that mirror. It warped far stronger men than him.

"You have something better," I tell him.

"What?"

"Me." I lean forward slightly. "I'm sure you've heard stories, Noctere. The stories your father told you might even hold a kernel more truth than the stories my mate heard. So you know I am quite capable at killing dragons. Do you doubt me?"

He swallows, then stares at me wide-eyed for a long moment. I decide to be patient; I suppose his entire worldview has been forced to shift. "No," he says finally.

"Good." I stand. "Let's end this, then. I have a mate waiting for me."

CHAPTER
TWENTY-FOUR

LEANA

Once I can't see Osir at all anymore, I venture into the cave.

I couldn't have imagined half as many jewels in the entire world. The whole cave glitters, every inch seemingly covered with piles of jewelry. All of it seems too grand for me to even look at, let alone touch. I feel the instinctive reaction to keep my hands firmly at my sides before I break something—or be accused of stealing it.

But I hear Osir's voice in my head, telling me this is mine now. That these are my jewels, that I have gone from a servant to the type of person who wears rubies.

There is a throne made entirely of gold against the cave wall, although why on earth Osir wanted that here and not in the castle throne room is a mystery. There are chests closed against one stone wall, and I curiously open one to find it positively stuffed with reams of silk, shimmering and light as butterfly wings, and lace, as delicate and intricate as spider silk.

What I could really use, I realize as I'm wandering through the piles of accumulated treasure, is food. I haven't eaten since before I left for the castle, and it feels like I burned through all my energy with my fire.

Of course, no food is forthcoming. If there ever was food here, it would have rotted away a century ago.

There is wine, but I ignore it. Knowing Osir, I'm sure it's very fine wine, but I think it's best for me to avoid that. I get a vision of me stumbling around drunk and destroying some prized possession of Osir's and shiver. Or worse, I could stumble outside to the sheer cliff-face and fall.

My stomach rumbles again as I set the bottle of wine down, the sound echoing off the cave walls.

What if this cave becomes my prison? I can't leave, after all, not without jumping to my death. Will someone bring me a bag of food once a week?

No. Osir wouldn't do that to me. This is temporary, and I can survive being hungry for a night.

Besides being hungry, I am bone-deep tired. I can feel it in every muscle, in every step. It's like I did a week's worth of hard chores in one go, burning out all my energy and exhausting my body.

I almost lie right on the ground, but once again I hear Osir in my mind, scolding me for passing up the opportunity for a better bed.

It feels wrong to unspool reams of silk and lay them on the ground, but I know he'd tell me to do it. I make myself a nest, and lay down to sleep, hoping that he'll be here when I wake.

***

I wake from a dream of Osir. In my dream, he came back to the cave. We were safe, and he'd slid into my makeshift bed right behind me, wrapping his arms around me to hold me close while we slept. He still hadn't managed to find any clothes.

I wake up alone, and somehow colder without his imaginary warmth at my back.

I stumble out to the ledge to see if I can spot him in the distance, some foolish hope blooming in my belly, but it's not yet dawn and I don't have a chance of spotting him.

I see smoke curling up into the sky. Is that the village Osir spotted yesterday, or has the attack spread further?

Either way, we are under attack, and Osir is the best person to handle it.

There's nothing else for it. I'll just have to ignore my twisting stomach. Osir will be back soon.

I almost clean up the fabric I made into a bed last night, but then I stop myself. Maybe Osir will be back soon. And he can change to his human form now, and...

I went so many years without worrying about things like this, but now I imagine him pushing me back into the pile of fabric. He'd follow me down, lying on top of me. And this time it wouldn't just be his words and my own touches that make me see stars. He'll be able to do it himself.

I close my eyes for a moment, remembering him telling me to imagine that my fingers against my throat, my breast, were his mouth. I'd give anything to feel that for real now.

I open my eyes, peeking behind me. But alas, my need for him didn't spontaneously summon him to me.

Even so, I leave the bed. Just in case.

Surely he'll be back soon. And while I dearly hope he doesn't intend to spend our lives in this cave, I have no objections to starting our lives together here.

In the meantime, I suppose I can continue to poke around his hoard. I have no doubt he was serious when he told me he wanted me to pick my favorite pieces.

His own two hands. He promised me he'd present me jewelry with his own two human hands, and that promise is about to come true.

There's more jewelry than I could ever know what to do with. There're thousands of pieces, probably, and I find my eyes physically incapable of taking them all in. I keep looking around at areas I know I've already looked over, and seeing new pieces like it's the first time I looked that way. It's simply unbelievable.

If he keeps calling this my hoard, I'm not going to know what to do with myself.

Wear it, I suppose. I think Osir would like that.

My eyes trail over diamonds and rubies, gold chains that could wrap around my neck a half dozen times and still likely have room to spare, silver so thin and spindly it looks like it will break with a touch. I don't dare pick any of it up, although I'm sure Osir would tell me it's mine to take.

I'm sure he'd say it, but that doesn't mean I quite believe it. Besides, I was serious when I said I'd only take his hoard from his two human hands.

In the furthest corner of the cave is a strange shape with a cloth over it. I stop, trying to place what it could possibly be. Everything else has been out and prominently displayed, except the fabrics which were presumably stored to preserve them. But what does a simple cloth preserve?

With Osir's voice reminding me that this is all mine echoing in my mind, I step over and pull the cloth away.

It's a mirror. It stands as tall as a man, with ornately carved gold edges. The glass itself looks tarnished, and I see cracks along the frame on one side. My breath catches, already realizing what this must be.

There's only one mirror Osir would consider worth keeping here. And there must be a reason he's so sure no one ever found his hoard, despite him being sure people looked for it. Because he knows they would have searched. And he knows that they never found the mirror.

The mirror Noctere sent me for is here. I hold my breath, watching the glass that's responsible for so many people's suffering.

The slightly tarnished glass grows so cloudy I can't see my own face, like someone is blowing smoke across the glass. "Who calls upon me?"

The voice echoes around the cavern, reverberating until it is loud enough to make me cringe. I don't answer. I certainly haven't called on it. I have no desire to talk to the mirror, and I debate throwing the cloth back over it.

"Speak, mortal," the woman's voice demands, shaking the room. An emerald necklace falls to the ground. "Who calls upon me?"

Do I call upon it? If it was my decision, I certainly wouldn't. But I fear she won't leave me alone until I speak, so I say, "My name is Leana."

"Leana," the mirror says, and the booming voice is replaced by an almost-gentle cooing sound. "Leana, I know your past and your future. Would you like a glimpse of it?"

"Do Osir and I get the life he promised me?" The question is out of my mouth before I can stop it. I want to know; I ache to know.

Let us get that life. Please.

His promises had once seemed so fantastical they bordered on cruel. Now I need them to survive.

The voice in the mirror hums infuriatingly, neither agreeing nor disagreeing. "Prove yourself worthy of my answers."

I have nothing that would show me as worthy of anything. I'm just Leana.

"I challenge you with a riddle, mortal. And if you can answer me truly, I shall show you everything you seek."

Do I really want to see what the mirror has to show? I remember everything Osir said about it. The damage it did, what it led him to do. His fear for his brothers, and Noctere, and the princes of Ashar. Perhaps I really should put the cloth back over it and hope it stops talking.

"If you wish to know how to secure your future with your mate, you'll need to answer me," the mirror warns, as if reading my mind.

I'm moving before I know what I'm doing, my hands wrapped around the frame. "Secure our future? Is something wrong?" I swallow. Perhaps it was selfish of me, but I never truly considered him in danger in this war. Dragons always seem so indestructible to me, and Osir seems particularly so.

I thought the hard part was over when I melted his chains. I thought our future was secure—that the only thing that could go wrong now would be if he came to his senses and changed his mind, although I've started to think even that wouldn't happen.

I've grown spoiled and content, and I should have known better. Something can always go wrong.

"Give me your riddle, then," I say in a rush. "I'll answer it."

How could I say anything else? If Osir is in danger, I need to know. What if this damn mirror tells me he's not coming back? That the future he convinced me could be real ended before it began?

"In hearts, I find my place to dwell.

A guiding light, I cast my spell.

To wield me right, a noble art.

But beware how I can break a heart.

What am I?"

The voice resonates around the cave, bouncing off the walls until every word has an echo, and I have to strain to fully understand what's being said.

A guiding light. I know what Noctere and Osir told me about this mirror. He said it will show whoever looks into it their path to true power. So if the answer is something that creeps into your heart, a guiding light to wield, then it must be power. That would be the only logical conclusion, right?

But it seems too easy. It seems almost like a decoy answer, and there's a much more fitting one buried in the riddle.

Break a heart. I suddenly know the answer. "Compassion," I say. I try to stand straighter, to tilt my head up, to act like I'm confident in this answer.

Compassion is the thing that creeps into your heart and acts as a guiding light. It is noble and right. But being compassionate, being kind, can break your heart.

I think of Noctere, who I once childishly might have called a friend. Who tried to send me to die. And I think of Osir, who returned my compassion tenfold.

The mirror makes a humming sound. "Not an answer I've heard before. But not an incorrect one, either. Perhaps it's more correct than any other. You're an interesting mortal. What should you seek from me?"

"I thought you only showed people what would make them powerful."

"If power is all someone seeks, it's all I show them. What do you seek, compassionate one?"

"Osir," I say immediately. "Please. Tell me—will he be okay? Will we be okay?"

The foggy mist behind the screen fades away, and suddenly I see myself lying in a bed as large and fluffy as any I ever saw in the castle. From the stone wall behind the bed, maybe it is the castle.

My hands are up by my head, gripping a pillow, and my mouth falls open into an oh. There's no sound, but I hardly need sound to figure out what's going on in the image.

Osir's head appears in view, resting on my stomach after he presumably crawls up from between my thighs. His face is wet, and he's grinning at me in a way I haven't seen on his human face yet. It's breathtaking.

I turn away from the mirror, unable to watch anymore without a stabbing longing building in my gut.

"So we get that. When is it?" I ask.

Osir will survive this war, then. But that could be years from now, for all I know.

"Soon."

Soon. It sounds wonderful until I remember that this mirror showed Osir a vision of power that never came true a century ago. Soon might not mean the same thing to the oracle as it does to me, a mere human.

"When?" I press, but I don't hear the answer before I hear something heavy land on the ledge outside.

Osir. This is my answer. Soon is now.

I think fleetingly of the pile of fabric I left out for exactly this purpose. I shiver, feeling my nipples tighten beneath my tunic. I want.

I run to the cave's entrance, only to find the small opening blocked.

There are four men there, all big and broad, with dragon scales clearly visible on their necks. I involuntarily take a step back, but they only advance closer.

"Your fucking mad king is plenty distracted now, pet," the one closest to me says. He's not the biggest of them, but I instinctively know he's the one to fear. His eyes are cold like death, a penetrating, brutalizing stare. His voice is practically a croon. It's not dissimilar to the voice Osir sometimes has when he's saying sweet, tempting things to me. But this voice doesn't feel soft and comforting like Osir's. It feels oily, like filthy slime dripping down my spine, and I cringe.

I take another step back, but the four of them only draw closer.

"Convenient of you to let him out of that hole," he says. "And good timing too, waiting until we were almost there. We were just going to torture this place out of him, but the two of you led us right here. And now he's left the poor human all alone," he says, the last words coming out with a mocking lilt. He takes another menacing step towards me, and I feel my heart in my throat.

He can't burn me, but that doesn't mean he can't hurt me. A dragon only needs a single claw or tooth to kill a human. He could step on me in that form. Even his human form could likely kill me, considering how strong he looks.

These are the warriors of Ashar Noctere tried to send me against. The ones I knew my fire wouldn't be enough to save me from.

And if I die, then so does Osir. I can't let that happen.

I force myself to bring my fire to my skin.

The one with eyes like death snickers. "Cute. But we're dragons, pet. Surely your mad king taught you a thing or two about us, before he locked the poor maiden away in his cave?"

"He'll come back for me." Whatever else might be true, I know Osir didn't do that. He'd never imprison me here.

He laughs outright now. "Oh, I doubt that, pet. Poor humans can't be expected to understand dragons. They're simple like that, aren't they?" he asks his companions, but doesn't wait for an answer. "You're a pretty enough treasure to him, I suppose. Surely you look good to a dragon who hasn't had company in a century. He's brought you back to his hoard, pet. You're no better than that necklace there. But even if he was so inclined, he's busy enough right now." He takes another step forward. "Speaking of treasure. We're here for a mirror. Don't get in our way and we'll let you live out the rest of your existence in this cave."

The damned mirror. Everything Osir said echoes in my head, and I know I can't let them have it.

I turn and run back to the other end of the cave, with their footsteps pounding right behind me. The only consolation I have is that this cave is too small for four dragons, but even in their human forms, they'll overtake me quickly.

But I don't need to get all the way there. I hurl fire at the mirror. Better to let it burn.

"No!"

I stop, chest heaving, barely able to catch a breath as it ignites. I squeeze my eyes shut for a moment, hoping it all burns.

But when I open my eyes, the mirror is still standing. The frame is singed, and the glass has soot stains, but it's clearly still functional.

The mirror is blank now, the scene I was shown having disappeared. Is the oracle simply done speaking to me, or did I just lose that future?

"You little bitch," one of them says, voice low and threatening. "This should teach you a lesson about playing with things you don't understand."

I can hear it behind me, and I turn just in time to intercept the ball of flame he sent my way. It melts into the flames still wreathing my arms, touching my outstretched hands and becoming part of me.

I glow so brightly I need to squint. This is the third time in two days I've been struck by dragon fire, and it feels like holding the sun every time. I thought I'd grow more used to it, but I feel like I'm the last little piece preventing the world from exploding, a plug barely holding the dam.

"Thank you for making this easy," I gasp, and then turn back towards the mirror, unleashing the full effect of the fire on it.

The blast knocks me backwards and blinds me completely, but I don't stop. I aim my hands where I think the mirror is, hitting it with every bit of fire in me. This is a job that needs to be done right. There can be no room for mistakes.

The fire leaves me in a trickle by the end, and I feel like I've been bled dry. I've never run out of fire before, and a part of me is missing. I'm nearly positive it will come back, but that doesn't stop the desperate, clawing feeling of wrong that it's gone now.

I gasp, pushing myself to my knees to see the damage I wrought, to see if I at least succeeded in my task.

The mirror is a pile of still-burning rubble, sharp, shiny shards poking out, still glowing red at the ends.

I did it. I rendered the mirror useless. I protected it like Osir wanted.

A hand closes on my shoulder, strong and clawed. "You fucking bitch," a deep, threatening voice rasps. "You think you're clever? You'll pay for that."

Then two hands are closing on my arms, and I have the presence of mind to struggle even though I know it will never help. With my fire burned out, I'm nothing. I could never hope to match the strength of a dragon.

His claws dig in, piercing skin, and I kick as he drags me to my feet, but he doesn't so much as flinch.

"Get the pieces," he snaps at the other soldiers. "We'll take them and her."

I squirm and kick again, but the dragon holding me just shakes me. "Knock it off, or I'll knock you out," he growls.

"Fuck!"

I forget to struggle, turning to the dragon trying to lift the still-glowing embers of the broken mirror.

"That bitch did something to it," he growls, turning from the mirror to stalk closer to me, cradling his hand to his chest. "I'll kill her."

"No. You won't." The dragon holding me has a voice like the coldest winter nights. "Do what I told you."

"I can't fucking lift it," he snaps back. "What do you suggest?"

"There's a chest over there. Go get it."

As the other dragon stomps off, my captor shakes me again. "What'd you do to it, huh?"

I feel a sharp glow of triumph, but it's short-lived as he shakes me again, clearly looking for an answer.

I might have done that, but my fire is gone now, depleted, and I have no hope of escaping this monster.

Osir.

I can't give in. I can't let him hurt me—not when I know what the consequences will be for Osir.

I start to struggle again.

I hear a sigh behind me, and then I'm released. I stumble, trying to move away from him, but before I can do anything, his hands wrap around my throat. "I warned you," he says, and then squeezes.

Chapter Twenty-Five

LEANA

I wake up flying again, and this time, I can't stop myself from vomiting.

The dragon holding me shakes me so hard my head snaps around. "Fucking bitch," he growls.

I dare look up. The dragon is large and ice blue, and while I can't be sure, I'm almost positive that this is the first dragon who spoke to me in the cave.

"Where are you taking me?" I make myself ask.

I get shaken again, and, mercifully, I pass out.

***

I wake up when something cold closes around my neck.

"What is it?" I ask hazily, opening my eyes but only getting a fuzzy view of the world.

Something clicks.

"There we go. A pet on a leash."

The cold voice wakes me up. "You're making a mistake," I tell him, raising a hand to feel the chain he's just locked around my neck.

He chuckles. "I don't make mistakes, pet."

"Who are you?"

"I'm Frost, a prince of Ashar. And you're in my home, for now."

I look around. We're in a small room, made entirely of stone with no furniture. There's a window high on a wall, letting in some weak sunlight as well as cold, frosty air.

It's a cell.

I'm not a dragon. I don't need a cave deep underground and enchanted cuffs. A chain and a locked cell will hold me just as well.

"What do you want with me?" I ask.

"If you hadn't gotten in our way, I would have left you alone," he murmurs. He grips my chin and tilts my head, so I'm forced to look at him. "I would have left your mad king his pet. But you broke what I wanted."

"That damned mirror?" I ask.

He growls. "That damned mirror that I orchestrated an entire war for," he says, the softness gone entirely from his

202

voice. "I did everything for a chance at it. Convinced my brother that if Dalyus won't give him a share, then he can take from that foolish, weak prince of yours. Researched and researched, found that stupid prison. And you broke it."

His grip on my chin gets tighter and tighter as he continues speaking, squeezing my face until I cry out in pain. He holds on for one extra moment, proving his point, before he releases me, only to caress my face.

"You didn't deserve it," I spit, and the hand on my face turns from a caress to claws pricking into my skin before I can breathe.

I try to bring forth my fire. I know it won't hurt him, but it might at least show him that I'm someone he doesn't want to hurt.

Nothing happens. I feel empty in a way I never have before, that I never knew I could. It would feel just as strange if my arm was cut off, I think.

I have no fire. I'm defenseless, all alone, and Osir has no idea where I am.

His hand moves from my face, leaving little biting pinpricks behind. I should have known better. I've always known that you never argue with a dragon, never argue with those with power. Only Osir has ever welcomed my honesty.

If I want to survive, I need to forget everything I became with Osir.

"Deserve doesn't have anything to do with the mirror, pet. The mirror is about power. It's about force. You think I can't force this?" When I don't respond, he huffs. "You break it, you fix it," he says evenly, and then moves aside to show me what his body was blocking.

Behind him is a pile of broken mirror shards, still red-hot at the edges, left in a mound on my cell floor.

"Fix it yourself." I look away, trying to ignore the broken shards.

He makes a soft sound and grabs my face, tilting it right back to where he wants it. "Whatever you did to it—no one else can touch it. So you're going to fix it for me."

"I won't." I try to sound resolved, sure. I try to remember how Osir sounded, still kingly even after years in chains.

It comes out weak, my voice wobbling. But I can't fix this for him. I can't give him that kind of power.

"You will if you like living." His words are cold and leave no room for interpretation. His mouth twitches into a cold smirk. "Be a good pet, and do as you're told."

Chapter Twenty-Six

OSIR

When dragons go to war, humans pay the price.

I know that better than anyone alive, the guilt of the hundreds and hundreds who were casualties of my brothers' and my squabble resting heavily inside me.

I don't even know the number we killed.

So for the past two days, I have used our forces to move attacks away from villages. I don't know if it's Leana's voice in my head pushing me to do it or my own guilt, and I don't care to examine it; neither option says good things about who I am as a person or a ruler.

I will do better now, I vow to myself, determined to protect as many human lives as possible.

The one thing I can say is that the troops from Ashar are not as fearsome as Leana had been led to believe. Nor are they as many.

Lorcate takes on half a dozen on her own, and I can hear her vicious laughter as she tears through them.

When the survivors of Lorcate's and my rage scamper off, flying back to the border like their tails are on fire, I land and turn back to my human form, cuffing my nephew around the arm before he can get away.

"We need to plan, nephew."

He squirms in my grip, reaching for the bag of clothes he wears tied around his ankle. But that's a useless waste of time, so I just tighten my hold. "What plan?"

I jerk my head to the retreating dragons. "That's not an army. That's a scouting party, perhaps. Or a targeted strike, meant for a particular assassination."

He stops fighting my hold. "They were meant for me?"

Likely, and we'd just intercepted them early. They hadn't expected competent resistance.

Truth be told, they weren't all that competent themselves. If they are the new king of Ashar's first line of attack, then perhaps Ashar is weaker than we thought.

Noctere tries to shake out of my grip again, and then he starts hyperventilating, face going pale. "I didn't ask for this," he murmurs.

"No? Well, you got it." I shake him. I should have more pity for him. But he threatened Leana.

And she asked me to help him, I remind myself. The thought sits like curdled milk in me, but that doesn't make it less true.

Leana helped me, and she wants to help him. She's kind like that, and I won't disrespect her kindness.

"We're going to end this," I tell him. "You're coming with me."

I drop his arm and turn back into my dragon form, then take off after the dragons we just sent running.

***

Noctere has the courage to follow me, which I admit is a little surprising. I push fast to follow our enemies, but he keeps up admirably, deftly moving so he's flying alongside me.

I look him over. In the air, I can almost forget how unsteady and unsure he seems on the ground.

A castle comes into view, and the three retreating dragons land there. I hang back, and Noctere follows my lead.

"What now?"

"Whose castle is that?" I ask.

He looks around for a long moment, and I brace myself for him telling me he doesn't know. But then he says, "Carus. The—"

"Second youngest brother, yes. You sure?"

"If we're where I think we are and our intelligence is correct. How did you know which brother he was?"

I snort. "Not everyone is as young as you, nephew. All four of the brothers were born before I was locked away, although the youngest was an infant. I remember things."

"Oh." He flaps his wings hard for a second. "Are we going down there?"

"No. Let's see how good your intelligence is. Let's go find the king."

***

Dalyus is not a young dragon, but he is a young king. The crown still sits awkwardly on his head, and I think for half an inane moment that he and my nephew might get along.

His people try to welcome us like this is a state visit of some sort, but I won't have it. I barely gave into the need to dress before marching into the throne room; I'm not here to be this king's friend.

I look at where the king sits on his paltry throne and bare my teeth. "Your brother betrays you."

He blinks. "Which brother?"

There's a certain eagerness in his tone. A certain desperation, maybe.

So he knew, and he just needed someone else to do the dirty work for him.

Noctere puffs himself up, and I brace myself for him to say something stupid. But all he says is, "We chased invaders from our land. They burned villages. Killed my citizens. And we followed them back to Carus' estate."

I watch the king, expecting some sort of "That's impossible!" or "Not my brother!" but nothing comes.

He knows. He just didn't know which brother betrayed him.

"We've heard whispers of war for months now," Noctere continues. "Skirmishes, incursions on our border. Testing our forces. And now we know who launched it."

"The only question remaining is, were those attacks sanctioned by you?" I ask, voice low, the threat obvious. Several advisors twitch around us, unsure if they need to defend their king.

But the king just slumps on his throne. "No," he mutters. If I weren't a dragon, I doubt I'd even hear it. "There's been unease since I took the throne. And since my brothers got their holdings. I just didn't know who..." He looks up at us, and his eyes turn to Noctere, pleading. I don't know why he looks to Noctere instead of me; maybe he thinks he'll get more sympathy from him. "There's been unrest here, too."

So Dalyus has a traitor in his midst and hasn't done anything about it.

Am I surrounded by incompetent rulers?

Then again, I thought I was so capable of ruling until I got hundreds of my citizens killed and was locked away as a result. So perhaps I should practice some patience.

But not that much patience. People will die if action isn't taken. And it won't be the dragon nobility in this room who pay the price.

Besides, I have a beautiful mate waiting for me, and I won't let their incompetence delay my return to her.

"Deal with your brother," I say lowly. "Or I will."

Dalyus just looks at me for a moment, then Noctere. "I'm sorry, who are you? I thought he…"

Noctere's mouth sets into a thin line, but then his eyes spark with some sort of determination. "Our kingdom works better as a council," Noctere says. "Once you root out your traitor, you should try it."

The idea is absolutely ludicrous, given how our last council had ended. My brothers dead, Braxil and I permanently estranged. But no one is laughing. No one is even arguing.

I take my nephew's bicep and turn him to face me. "Are you sure?" I murmur, well aware every dragon in the room can hear me, anyway.

Noctere's eyes still look determined. "What, do you not want it?"

Oh, I want it. But I know the concession it will be for my nephew.

I don't let on, though. He's made his choice. "Leana will be ruling at our side," I tell him simply, straightforward, not leaving any room for negotiation.

If Leana decides she does want him dead, him having publicly claimed me as his co-ruler in front of so many will only benefit Leana and I in the long run. I'll have a throne to offer her, and perhaps minimal bloodshed to get there.

I find myself hoping she doesn't want him dead, though.

Speaking of my mate, I feel an itching under my scales, like now that I've come this far, I'm being driven to go to her.

Well, that's fine by me. I much rather be with her than be here.

"Can you see this done?" I ask Noctere.

He looks back up at Dalyus, who's watching us with bemusement, and nods. "Go find her. Can you tell her I'm sorry?"

That's pushing things a step too far. "Tell her yourself," I say, turning and leaving the room, already forgetting Ashar and their problems, only thinking about my mate.

***

I think about her the whole way back to my hoard. If I was at my best as a king, I'd scan the countryside, looking for any more threats. But I could hardly care; my mind is fully focused on my mate.

Leana. She was so sensitive when she touched herself in my prison. Could I make her moan like that? Could I make her scream?

I'll have the whole night to find out how to make her desperate for me.

What I will need is a place to bring her for the night, and I break off picturing her pert breasts to scan the land below me. I don't think I'm above kicking some petty lord out of their house for the night.

But that's when I smell it. More smoke.

Smoke from dragon fire, yes. But also Leana's fire.

What in the world could she be burning?

I push myself faster, but the smell only grows stronger when I get closer to my hoard.

I land on the ledge with a jarring thump, changing to my human form without hesitation.

The cave looks like a drunk dragon ambled through it, knocking things every which way. Half of my beautiful treasures are in disarray. And there's no sign of my mate, who would outshine every single treasure.

The smell of smoke is inescapable, and tearing my eyes away from a ruby necklace that I can't help picturing around Leana's beautiful throat tells me why.

The back half of the cave is burned. Burned by Leana, no doubt.

I know what was back there. My heart thumps wildly, remembering where I'd placed that cursed mirror.

Did Leana find it and melt it on purpose? Did seeing the object that did so much damage prove to be the final straw?

I shake my head to dislodge the stupidity. No. Leana is gone, and she couldn't have left on her own.

There's dragon fire here.

There were dragons here.

And they took my mate.

CHAPTER TWENTY-SEVEN

LEANA

I turn my head to the side as the door creaks open, letting in a bright light from the hallway.

"You can come back as often as you want, it won't change my answer," I tell him listlessly, unable to summon the energy to really argue with him. I feel washed out and empty inside, and every time he visits, it's like the life drains out of me even faster.

"You make this harder on yourself," he tells me, stepping fully into the room and closing the door behind him. It's a formality. It's probably meant more for intimidation than practicality. It's not like I can leave—the thick collar and chain around my neck sees to that.

No, he does it to prove a point. That he has me here, that he controls everything, and that, if he wanted to, he could hurt me very badly.

I close my eyes instead of responding to him. What's the point? What can I say?

Yes, I'm making this hard on myself, but I don't know what else to do.

I've barely been fed, haven't been allowed to bathe or change clothes, and the bucket they gave me for a toilet reeks in the corner of the room.

And then there's Frost, who grows closer and closer to real violence every day he comes in here. I can feel it brewing under his skin, every time he looks at me.

One day, he's going to realize I won't fix the mirror. And then he'll kill me.

I need to hope that day is as far off as possible. Not for my own life, but for Osir.

Because I'm not an idiot. Frost will kill me the second the mirror is re-made. I just need to hope that Osir can find me before Frost gets fed up with me ignoring him.

Osir, if you're out there... please.

He grabs the chain secured to my neck and jerks it sharply. I gasp for air, reaching up to my throat. The sharp jerk of the chain pulls me down, and I land on my elbows, scraping them bloody on the stone. The sting of pain makes my eyes prick, but I bite my lip to stop it from showing.

I can't react. I can't show that he's hurt me, scared me. That's what he wants.

I slowly open my eyes and look up at him. He towers above me, no doubt trying to remind me of my place.

"Listen when I'm talking," he says simply, like we were having a simple conversation, like he's in any place to remind me to be polite.

"Sorry," I rasp, the words hurting coming out of my surely bruised throat. "What were you saying?"

He stares at me for a long moment before answering. "There are ways to make this easier on yourself. If you fix it, then I can improve your circumstances."

I don't reply. I doubt the mirror can even be properly fixed, although I suppose we'll never know unless I try, because he's convinced I'm the only person who can touch it.

We both know I'm not going to fix the mirror. And I want to shout it at him, to tell him to go fuck himself. But I bite my tongue and don't acknowledge him.

I think it hurts him more than anything I could actually say, so I take some small pride in that.

***

I don't get fed. There's a cup of water, and I gulp it down greedily before it's taken away.

The still-glowing embers of the mirror cast an eerie glow around my cell, but at least I'm not left in darkness.

My flames still haven't returned. I've never actually been at risk of being left in the dark before now.

I don't know why they're gone. Maybe absorbing dragon fire to do the things I did three times in a matter of days was simply too much. Maybe there was something about Frost's flames that destroyed my own. Maybe my flames will eventually come back, and I just need to give it time.

Every night I hope that they'll be back by morning, and every morning I'm disappointed. It's a soul-deep emptiness, like something critical was removed. I doubt I'd feel any different if someone pulled out my heart and I somehow went on living.

What would I do if it was back tomorrow? Flames aren't enough to fight a dragon.

But they might be enough to burn a castle. And I doubt that this chain on my neck is enchanted, so my own fire could probably melt it.

And as for fighting a dragon? My flames would never be enough. But I look at the still-burning shards of mirror, and wonder if any of them are particularly sharp.

Chapter Twenty-Eight

OSIR

I storm back into Dalyus' throne room, daring anyone to get in my way.

People scatter before me, and I don't stop until I arrive at the base of the throne, looking around for someone to blame. "Who took her?" I demand, my voice low with a barely suppressed threat. I am ready to kill anyone who gets in my way. My whole body vibrates with my pent up and barely checked rage.

"Took who?" the king asks me. He's not looking at me directly, and I realize distantly I ignored all social niceties of re-dressing. I can't be bothered to care.

"My mate," I snarl, ready to unleash on him. I don't think he took her, but right now I don't much care to be discerning with my targets. "Who took my mate?"

"Leana is gone?" Noctere demands, appearing at my side.

"Gone. Someone burned her and took her."

Dalyus makes an awkward throat clearing noise. "Someone burned her? Osir, I'm sorry, but she's—"

"She's not dead," I snap, because at least I know that much. She's not dead, because I won't survive her leaving this world. I'll follow her within a heartbeat and be glad for it. "She can survive fire."

"She can," Noctere confirms. "She's powerful." He turns back to me. "Anything else?"

I don't want to mention the mirror in front of them. I shake my head. "No. She's gone. It had to be one of your princes. Just another way to destabilize our kingdom."

I'm still alive, I remind myself. I'm still alive, so she must still be alive.

Noctere seems to be thinking along the same lines. "You couldn't have mated her?" he mutters to me. "Given her a better chance?"

"You couldn't have held the kingdom together as king for one day to give me time to do so?" I snap back. It's unfair, but I'm not in the mood to be fair.

I want Leana. Here, now. Safe in my arms. And anyone I have to hurt along the way is irrelevant.

"Roso is already here," Dalyus says, ignoring our heated words. "He came as soon as we sent out the call. I don't believe he had anything to do with encroaching on your kingdom, or your mate."

He gestures broadly as he speaks, and I take in the man he points to. Roso is almost seven feet tall, and burly enough to crush skulls without transforming into his dragon form. But he stands calmly by, watching all of this, and shrugs when I make eye contact with him.

"I have my territory. I have a role in this court. I'm satisfied." He pauses for a moment. "You told my brother Carus led the incursions?"

"Yes," I say, voice clipped, not in the mood to debate.

He nods slowly. "Carus has always been ambitious. Frost too. We'll see what they say."

***

Roso's territory is right outside his brother's keep, but word takes longer to make it to the others. I'm left waiting for three agonizing days, and at every moment I want to fly off.

Noctere stops me each and every time. "Easy," he murmurs. "Ashar is a big place. You can't just sniff her out, Osir."

Trying would be more useful than sitting here.

Roso and Dalyus want to discuss a treaty between our nation and theirs, but I don't want to discuss peace when I don't know if there can be peace.

If a single hair is harmed on Leana's head, I'll kill whoever is responsible, and damn the consequences. I'll burn this entire kingdom to ash, if that's what it takes.

Finally, late in the afternoon of the third day, word comes that the youngest prince has arrived.

He strolls in like he owns this castle, and I want to throttle him for his arrogance, for not understanding the gravity of the situation. "Carus is dead," he announces, not waiting for any greetings.

The air feels heavy and still. "Dead?" Roso checks.

"He was trying to flee. I stopped him," Frost says. He holds his head high and keeps his gaze even, but I tense.

Liar. Filthy, filthy liar.

Roso growls. "We needed to know how deep his conspiracy goes."

Dalyus sighs, rubbing a hand over his face. "The traitor is dead, Roso. We'll live with that."

They squabble amongst themselves for a few minutes, and I look at my nephew. He's watching the proceedings with a frown.

Good. He can feel it, too.

Noctere clears his throat. "Did you investigate his keep?"

Frost barely looks him over. "I was there."

"Was my uncle's mate there? Human, dark hair, her name is Leana."

He doesn't deign to face us again. "No."

No, she wasn't there. I could have already guessed that.

I approach the throne. "We'll leave you to your business, and we'll go home to ours," I say gruffly to Dalyus. "We'll meet in a week to discuss this treaty further?"

If Dalyus finds my sudden acquiescence to a treaty strange, he doesn't say anything. He nods absently, but not before I turn to the youngest brother.

Who certainly smells like my mate.

***

"Go home," I tell Noctere, standing around outside Dalyus' castle.

He raises an eyebrow. "And what will you do?"

"I'll get my mate back," I tell him.

"And that's not a two dragon job?"

I refrain from mentioning that Noctere would not be my first choice for help when it comes to a fight. "Go home. Make sure things are running smoothly. Make a plan for rebuilding those villages. I'll be there soon."

He looks at me for a long moment, but he does leave, giving me plenty of time to plan.

By the time the youngest prince leaves and turns into his dragon form—an ice blue dragon, as cold as his heart—all I know is one thing: I am going to get my mate back. I won't go one more night without her.

Chapter Twenty-Nine

LEANA

As Frost suspected, the mirror shards don't burn me when I touch them. In fact, it feels a little bit like they're the pieces of myself that have been missing since I was taken. It's like their heat supplements my heat, warm and inviting.

I carefully look the pile over, searching out shards big enough for me to grab, with hopefully at least one non-sharp side so I don't slice my hands open. When I think I identify two pieces, I pick them up.

They crumble to dust in my hands.

But even as they crumble, I can feel the fire inside me again.

It's like the burning mirror shards get absorbed into my hands, like the fire transfers from them to back inside me.

I gasp in relief. My fire. Back where it belongs.

The listless, despondent feeling that's curdled my insides for days fades away, and I smile to myself.

There's no oracle to tell me how to get out of here. But that's okay. I've begun to figure it out for myself.

When I'm left with a pile of ash and fire thrumming under my skin, I know it's time to make my escape.

I wish I had a weapon. I'm more than glad to have my fire back, but it won't scare off a dragon. Then again, few weapons a human could wield would scare off a dragon. I'm more liable to hurt myself than my captors.

I force myself to take a deep breath. I'll have to do the best I can with what I have.

I wrap my hand around the collar on my neck, and shudder when I think of Osir being chained for an entire century.

The metal breaks under the heat of my hands, and I fling it away, watching the half-melted mess clatter into the pile of ashes from the mirror.

Good riddance to all of it. To that infernal collar and to that mirror, and all the fighting and death it caused. To this damn castle and this war.

I light the door on fire.

I've never tried stepping through fire before. I know it can't hurt me; I've let fire touch every inch of my skin, I've stuck my hand in fires, and I've faced dragon fire and walked away. But there seems to be a world of difference between knowing this and allowing myself to walk through a wall of fire.

I close my eyes and take a deep breath. The point is to escape, and if I don't do this, it's all for nothing.

If I don't do this, then I can say goodbye to the future I saw in the mirror.

I take it at a run, bursting through the flames. When I feel the heat at my back, I open my eyes and turn to look.

The wood door has burned away, and the fire will spread soon. I decide to help it along, bringing my flames to the surface, letting them burst from my skin. The flames come immediately, naturally, like they were just waiting for me to call them.

They seem more active than I remember. My flames have always responded immediately to my call, but they were under my control, passive to my demands. Now they feel ready to jump right off my skin, like they could flare as bright as the sun at any moment.

I look at my white-hot hand. Maybe that's a good thing. Maybe that's what this castle deserves.

When I walk down the hall, I attempt to touch everything I can.

I was unconscious when they dragged me into this castle, so I have no idea how to escape. I keep walking, keep letting the fire spread, and try not to think about what I'll do when I get outside.

I've never even seen a map of Ashar. I couldn't begin to guess where in the kingdom I am, or how far it is away from my home. Will I need to walk for weeks?

Then I'll walk for weeks, I think sternly, and light a heavy, ornamental drape on fire.

At last, I turn a corner and see a heavy door at the end. I pick up speed, determined to make it to freedom.

I have a feeling Osir and I will be spending a lot of time outside in our future. I doubt either of us is going to be particularly enthused about closed rooms.

With conscious effort, I force my flames back beneath my skin. I don't want to burn the door down, I remind myself. I'm not a monster, and I have no idea who is in this castle. People might need to escape.

I push the heavy door open, wincing at the creak, although I suppose there's no chance of anyone hearing that over the crackling fire and chaos behind me.

But when I slip outside, I realize with a sinking stomach that being silent didn't make a single difference. Because my enemy can see me.

"You bitch," Frost hisses, walking towards me, his eyes promising a slow death.

I step back until I hit the door, and then summon the flames to my skin.

"That won't work on me," he growls.

I swallow. I know, but I also know it's all I have. So I square my shoulders, look him in the eye, and make the flames glow a little brighter.

Chapter Thirty

OSIR

The glowing skyline is a beacon, and I push myself harder than I likely ever have before. There. She must be there.

I'd had to let the prince get ahead of me, lest he catch on to being followed. Every moment I let him grow smaller in the distance made my heart beat faster. If I let him make it to his home before me, what would he do? Would he hurt Leana?

Would these few minutes be all he needs to kill her?

But then flames illuminate the night, and it calls to me like a siren's song.

Is she waiting for me? Is she signaling me with the fire, knowing I needed just a sign, a single clue, to find her?

I'm in the northern reaches of Ashar, the region under the control of the youngest brother. There's little here besides ice, the single castle standing out like a stark figure against the white backdrop.

Or it would, if it wasn't on fire, with an entire wing already starting to crumble.

A fierce surge of pride rips violently through me. That's my mate. My Leana, my greatest treasure, who was too scared to ignore royal protocol even in a cell, has now burned down a castle.

She's a queen of flames, and I will spend every day reminding her of that.

I follow the fire to its brightest point, crashing down into the snow-covered ground to take in the scene.

She's here. She's here, at the center of a blaze, here and real and alive.

I want to go to her. I want to be consumed by her flames, even if they hurt.

Dragons don't fear fire. We revel in it. And I want to revel in her.

But there's someone else present, someone to ruin our reunion. I turn my attention to him reluctantly, not wanting to take my eyes off of her for a second.

But I have a duty as her mate to ensure she is safe.

"You dare threaten what's mine?" I growl, stalking closer. My huge limbs eat up the distance between us. Leana is a bright, burning ball out of the corner of my eye, so much brighter than the crumbling castle.

I snarl. "You dare harm my mate? My treasure?"

He stole her from me. Imprisoned her. No doubt scared her, hurt her in ways I ache to think about. And now I see this.

If she's burning like this, then he must have tried to burn her. And he no doubt discovered that such a thing is entirely ineffectual, but it's the fact that he did it. That he was so willing to hurt her.

Leana, who doesn't hurt others. Who is kind and compassionate, who fed a dragon she truly believed deliberately massacred people like her. Who spoke to me and sat with me, who gave me a chance. Who advocated on behalf of Noctere, despite him never being kind to her. Who is goodness personified.

He hurt her, and he's invited his own death by doing so.

I'd hoped Leana would never see me like this, as this creature of violence. I'd hoped she'd consider the dragon form to be a protector, not a killer. I'd hoped I could fight for our kingdom and then bring her home in safety, with her not having to see a single moment of the violence.

But this is not something we can avoid. As the dragon who cornered her begins to transform, I move between the two of them, carefully putting Leana at my back.

"Leana," I growl. "I need you to run, treasure."

I hear her scrambling to move out of our way, and then I'm forced to tear my attention from her, focusing entirely on the blue dragon before me.

"You really want that witch?" he asks, and I think if he was still in his human form, he'd be smirking at me. "Look what she did."

I don't turn to look, but I do feel the heat of the fire at my back. And all it does is bring me pride.

Look at my queen. Look what she can do.

I asked the oracle to show me true power. And that mirror was absolutely right. Leana is the most powerful creature I've ever seen.

"My queen will burn down your little castle. And I will bring her home and worship her for it."

And then I attack.

He holds his ground for a few moments, even managing to rake his claws through my scales. But I have something to fight for.

Leana, ripped away from me, stolen from a place where I promised she was safe. Leana, who should be home in our castle, treated like the queen she is, already wearing the treasure I've tucked away in my bag. Leana, who must have been so scared.

I want to make him suffer, but I want to go to my treasure more, so with one final swipe of claws and teeth, I take out his throat and end the threat.

I shift back to my human form, left naked and dripping blood from my hands and mouth. I wish I didn't have to approach Leana like this. I wish I didn't have to show her this part of me—

Strong arms wrap around me, and I freeze for a second before lifting Leana off the ground, holding her tight to me as I bury my face in her hair.

My treasure, in my arms once more. My world feels whole again.

I could stay right here forever, but I need to ensure that she's all right. I pull back and vaguely register that she's not burning anymore before I look the rest of her over.

She's dirty, and I very much doubt it's all soot from the fire. There are bruises around her neck.

I tilt her head and watch her shiver under my fingers. That's a reaction I'd very much like to note for later, but right now I force myself to study her bruises.

Not like fingers gripping her. Like a collar, or a chain. Something big and abrasive that rubbed and tugged at her delicate skin.

A growl works up through me, sounding as fierce as anything that comes out of my much larger dragon form. "Tell me who else hurt you," I demand. "Tell me so I can kill them too."

She reaches for me, grabbing at my shoulders and pulling me back into her. I go willingly enough, letting her body pressing against mine soothe the dragon calling for blood.

She doesn't need to see that. She clearly doesn't want to see that.

"I took care of it," she says, voice muffled by my chest. "Look."

I have no desire to look at anything but her ever again, but I know what she's referring to. The castle, crumbling under fire.

I press kisses on the top of her head. There's soot and dirt in her hair, but I couldn't care less. "My brilliant treasure. Look what you can do."

"I couldn't do that before. Not this much, not this quickly."

"He used his dragon fire on you, didn't he?" I ask. "Like Noctere's soldier did. That's why you could do it."

"No. Well, yes, but—days ago. When he first took me. It's how I destroyed the mirror."

I freeze. "You destroyed the mirror?"

Why hadn't I tried to do that? Why hadn't I offered incontrovertible proof to my brothers that it was destroyed and ended the whole violent fight for it?

I know why. Because I am as selfish as everyone else who ever came in contact with the mirror. Because I wanted what it promised.

And here is Leana, brilliant, beautiful Leana, stronger than me, stronger than anyone.

"I didn't want him to have it," she whispers into my chest. "And when he attacked me for trying to burn it on my own—I used his fire to destroy it." Her fingers, still digging into my shoulder blades, tighten. "But he brought the pieces, and they kept burning. He wanted me to put them back together, and when I touched them—it was like I got all the fire back. And then, well, you can see what I did."

I certainly can. I look up for half a second to see what she managed to do, then look back at her. She's infinitely more worth watching than a burning castle.

My mind spins, thinking of the implications of what happened with the mirror. But I push the thought away. The researcher part of me wants to know, but that part is buried deep, deep down, hidden underneath all the parts of me clamoring for my mate.

I take a deep breath, inhaling her scent under the smoke and soot and dirt. "I know you didn't enjoy flying," I tell her, "but it's time we return home, wouldn't you say?"

CHAPTER THIRTY-ONE

LEANA

F lying with Osir is infinitely better than flying with Frost, but that's like saying I'd rather have a broken limb than an amputation. Neither option is especially appealing.

I know, given everything that's happened recently, that flying home is the last thing I should complain about. But I still feel like my stomach is trying to escape the entire way. So I keep my eyes firmly squeezed shut, trying to think about anything else.

I think about Osir's human form holding me close when he found me, after he killed Frost. I think of his warm body, strong and powerful.

I think of him not looking at anything but me, the way he said my name, the way he touched me, so gentle, so desperate. The way he called me his treasure.

I don't think anything ever sounded sweeter.

I even think of the way he held me, still dripping in blood. I couldn't care less. If I'd been asked previously, I'm sure I would have said I'd find it disgusting.

He killed Frost for me. He killed Frost to protect me, to avenge me. And he threatened to kill anyone else who hurt me, too.

Despite what the kingdom has believed for a century, I know Osir's first instinct isn't violence. But I also know that he'll never let anyone hurt me ever again.

I shiver at the memory, feeling irrationally pleased that my mate would do that for me. Then, I go back to remembering what it was like to be held close in his human arms, and the thoughts are almost enough to chase off the nausea.

***

When Osir lands in the courtyard of the castle, he sets me down gently and immediately transforms back to a man, ignoring the small group that rushes outside at our arrival.

Osir just growls at them and takes my hand, tugging gently on my arm to pull me into his side. He seems completely unselfconscious about his nudity, despite our small audience.

I go willingly, leaning against him. He's so warm against me, and it makes me feel heated in a different way than any fire ever has. Will it always be like that?

"Your majesty, I—"

Osir stops for a moment and turns to the man who spoke, growling. "As you can see, I have found your queen and killed the bastard who stole her from us. No one is to disturb your queen and I for three days. If Ashar attacks, deal with it yourself. If the plague strikes, we'll learn about it when we emerge. If the sun doesn't rise tomorrow, it is not our problem. If the castle is on fire, assume we are enjoying the flames and leave us be. Do not so much as think about us until we emerge." He pauses for half a second. "And we'll need food. Lots of it. Leave it outside the door."

He doesn't give them time to respond, just tugging gently on my hand again, pulling me down a corridor.

"Queen?" I manage to squeak, stuck on that word. It's easier to address that than the sharp, pleasurable tingles inside me from the rest of what he said.

"I always said you were a queen, treasure. Now they know it too. There's still issues to resolve, but yes—you will be queen. And there has never been a better one, I'm sure." He brings our clasped hands to his mouth, kissing the back of my hand with infinite gentleness.

That really doesn't even begin to answer my question, but I lose focus when his lips touch my skin. "Where are we going?"

He stops entirely, then turns fully to me. He looks me in the eye and I suddenly have a strong idea where we're going. I see us in bed, getting a flash of his face buried in my neck, my head thrown back. I blink, and the image disappears, but I find myself hungry for it.

Without warning, he scoops me into his arms, holding me to him. I shriek at the sudden movement, but quiet when he kisses me.

Then I'm groaning into the kiss, using one hand to cup his jaw and hold him there.

He rests his forehead against mine. "I am going to bring my mate to bed," he whispers. "I am going to worship her as she deserves, show her how a mate loves their mate, and start our future together. If she lets me."

"She'll let you," I whisper back, shivering in anticipation. "Happily." I swallow. "Excitedly."

"Oh?" He rubs his nose on mine. "Are you excited for me, treasure?"

The question seems rhetorical, but I want to answer any-way. "I never thought... I never wanted..." I huff in frustration when the words don't come. "Osir, I'm honored to be your mate. Please—please show me how good it'll be. Because you convinced me with just words when you couldn't even touch me, and now I want to know."

I never thought I'd do this. I never considered this the type of future I wanted.

But I want Osir, and badly. Every one of his words from the cave echoes in my mind, and I want him to prove them true.

Osir starts walking down the hallway, moving rapidly, clearly unable to wait any longer. "I'd be honored," he promises me, voice low. "No dragon ever had such a wonderful mate."

I'm sure all dragons say that. It makes me flush with pride, nonetheless.

I tilt his face back to mine. "Osir, this is it, right? We do this and we're bonded forever?"

"You already have me forever, treasure. Nothing in the world could change that. Nothing. I am yours until the end of time. Don't agree to this because you want to know I'm yours."

Dragons. Or maybe just my dragon. Honestly.

"What if I want to be yours until the end of time, too?"

"Then I'd ask you to do one more thing for me first."

"Anything." I mean it, too. I think I'd do anything he asks.

But only because I know he'd do anything for me.

He opens an ornate wooden door into a room I've never been in before. "My room," he explains, turning slightly so I can look around without him putting me down.

The room is sprawling, with an elegantly appointed sitting room by the fire, a small desk space, multiple bookshelves, and a bed with a thick, soft duvet and a dozen pillows that could fit every girl in my room upstairs easily, with room to spare.

Even the little details look like a type of luxury I could never imagine. There's art on the walls, lush countryside scenes and several seascapes. I have no doubt the rugs keep the floor warm and would be one of the softest things I'd ever felt. There are even vases of fresh flowers on the end tables.

But none of that is what catches my eye. The room has windows—with actual glass in them—looking out over a large garden, giving the space an open, airy feeling. There's another door between the windows, giving us private access to the garden.

"This was my room before. I spent significant time in my own land holdings, but when I was here, this is where I liked to be. It seemed appropriate to take it back."

It seems perfect. No more underground holes, or chains on the wall, or rough floors beneath us. No more misery.

I look at the windows once more. Perfect.

"There's a bathing chamber through there," he says, pointing past the fireplace. "I can show you later. And there's a closet, which I'm sure we can have filled with things for you in no time."

I realize then that I'm still wearing the clothes I washed without soap in the cave. They're sooty and burned and just plain filthy, and somewhere along the way I lost my old boots. "I could use a fresh set of clothes," I admit. These aren't good for anything more than rags, if they're even good for that, with how much muck is caked into them now.

"You'll have more than just a fresh set," he promises.

Osir has a very strange perception about what I actually need. "I don't need much more than one," I say. "I'm sure my other clean set of clothes is upstairs in my room."

"You won't need that again. You'll have the finest of everything."

I turn to face him instead of the room only to find that he's already watching me intently, a small, soft smile on his handsome face.

How often did I wonder what his face would look like? How often did I wonder what the smile I thought I heard in his voice would look like?

Breath-taking.

"I don't care about the finest of everything," I tell him. "I just want you. You know that, right? You. Not whatever you can give me."

I know I come from nothing, have nothing, but I need him to know that I didn't choose him because he could offer me a nice bed and a new dress.

I chose him because he cared. Because he listened to me, because he looks at me like I matter. Because he's sweet, and his words make me want to believe in the future he promises.

His eyes go even softer than before, and he moves to set me down so I'm seated on the edge of the bed. It's even softer than I thought, feeling like I'm sinking into a cloud.

Then he kneels in front of me, taking both of my hands in his. "I'm going to ask you to care about one thing I can give you."

I bite my lip. Is this an innuendo? But he seems so sincere, so I just nod my head.

As if that's the permission he needs, he reaches for a bag still tied to his ankle, untying it and pulling out a small parcel that he cups carefully in his large hands. He's more shy about whatever this is than he has ever been about nudity, looking like a timid child when he turns back to me.

"I think humans do rings," he says. "And I'll get you a thousand rings if you want them. But dragons—we give our mate the first piece in our hoard that reminds us of them. It's a sign of commitment, treasure, that I give and you accept."

He shows it to me then, the necklace he's been hiding in his hands. My breath catches. It's made of rubies secured with gold links, shiny and elegant looking.

"It reminds me of fire," he says softly. "The golds and the reds. Beautiful like you, of course. You will make it shine."

"I love it," I whisper, and it's true. It's too grand for me, perhaps. Too much. Far too precious. But I love that he loves it. That he saw it and thought of me. That he thinks it reminds him of my fire, that it's beautiful. That I will do it justice.

I lift my chin. I want to be the woman he sees when he thinks of this necklace. "Will you put it on me?"

"I would be honored," he says, voice hoarse. He uses one hand to sweep my disheveled hair off my neck, then frowns. "Those bruises... I don't want to hurt you."

"I can barely feel them." Not necessarily true, but I would say anything to get that necklace from him right now. I hold eye-contact with him, hoping he understands it, because I can already see myself wearing it, and I want that between us.

He frowns for a moment but concedes, sliding onto the bed behind me so he can fasten the necklace for me. When his fingers lightly brush the back of my neck, I shiver.

He groans. "Human hands are good for so many things." I hear the necklace clasp securely, and then it rests against the back of my neck. "Clasps, for instance."

I swallow. "What else?"

He kisses my neck, right above the necklace. "Oh, my mate wants more?"

I want to tell him that he made me climax in a cave with nothing more than just his words. I want to say he's made me promises that have driven me out of my mind, making me want to know if they're true. That he's filled most every thought of mine since that day.

I want to say that I have been hurt, threatened, and scared. That this type of intimacy was something to fear and something to avoid. That just his words have changed everything for me, and I want to know what his actions can do.

"I want you to see it first," he murmurs into my ear, his breath a hot tickle that makes me shudder.

"It?" I ask, too distracted by his closeness to even begin to know what he means.

He kisses my neck and I can feel that smile that I've so quickly become enamored with. "The necklace, treasure. I want you to see the necklace."

CHAPTER THIRTY-TWO

OSIR

Her breathing has picked up speed, making her little breasts bounce beneath her filthy ripped tunic. I need to get that off of her as soon as possible.

And then burn it immediately. It should never touch her skin again.

There's a flush on her face and neck now too, and I smile to myself, kissing from just over the clasp of the necklace to the hinge of her jaw, light, teasing kisses. I watch her hand fist on her thigh, squeezing.

But I want her to see this necklace on herself. I want her to see what I see.

It's a beautiful necklace, although it pales in comparison to her. But I have to accept that nothing would ever compare to her beauty. I could scour the earth for a thousand years and never find the perfect jewels for her. She will simply outshine them all.

With great reluctance, I slide off of the bed, standing in front of her and offering her a hand. "Come see."

She takes my hand, letting me help her to her feet. Her toes sink into the rug and she freezes.

"What is it? Are you okay?"

"It's even softer than I imagined," she whispers.

My throat tightens. It is soft, and I take it for granted. Well, so will she. There will be so many soft things in her life that she will simply come to expect them. And after tonight, she will have a long life left to live, filled with jewels and softness and love.

"Come," I murmur, squeezing her hand gently while guiding her to the other room.

We'll have to spend some time in here soon. I'll get my chance to be her bathing attendant like I promised myself in the cave. If it were any other circumstances, I'd ensure she gets a long, relaxing bath right this moment.

But right now, I need to do this properly. I need to take the steps to seal our mating.

Leana will have my protection. She will have the dragon to defend her physically and my long life to guard her. Nothing like what happened will ever be able to occur again.

There's a mirror on the wall, and I position her in front of it, stepping in behind her to crowd her body against mine. Perfect.

"Look at yourself," I murmur, reaching a hand up to move her hair from her neck. Her hair, as dark and beautiful as the midnight sky, really calls for diamond pins. And her little fingers call for rings, and her wrists for a thousand jingling bracelets.

And I will give her all of that, I remind myself. But first we're here, looking at the very first piece I've ever had the privilege of giving her.

Dragons tend to get ahead of ourselves, thinking about the next great thing and not appreciating the moment. I vow to appreciate this moment, and every moment, with my treasure.

"Look at the queen I am so lucky to call mine."

I expect her to demur, to brush me off. Instead, Leana sets her shoulders back and lifts her chin, showing off the necklace in the best possible light. She makes it look radiant, and I couldn't be more proud of her.

I lean down to kiss her neck. "My queen."

"I think I like treasure better," she admits, tilting her head so I can press more kisses to her neck, which I eagerly do.

"Oh?" I ask, nipping at her ear. "I suppose that makes sense. You're everyone's queen. But only my treasure." I lick at her skin and then blow across it, and I feel my cock hardening as she shivers. "My beautiful, perfect treasure."

"Yes," she whispers, and I know that this is my invitation.

I let myself put my hands on her, framing her ribcage, thumbs a daring inch away from the beautiful breasts I want to touch so badly. I want these clothes gone; I want her laid out under me, naked and panting and with want in her eyes—

I am so close to the future I dreamed of, of having everything I ever wanted. I run my thumbs over her skin, stroking back and forth, and bend my head so I can speak directly in her ear. "Do you want this?" I ask.

"Yes," she moans.

"Do you want me? Forever?"

"Yes. Osir, yes." She moves then, turning in my hold so she's facing me, and her hands come up to cradle my face. She pauses for a second, holding my eyes before pulling me into a kiss that I eagerly fall into.

Whether it's her hands on me or her saying my name in that breathy little voice, I couldn't begin to guess. But my mate wants me, and I lose all semblance of control.

Give her what she wants.

I grip the hem of her stained tunic and start to lift it, then force myself to stop. "I'll make you feel so good," I promise her, and I can hear the barely restrained desperation in my voice. "I'll worship you like you deserve, treasure. And you'll tell me what you like, hm?"

"I don't know what I like," she says, her hands trying to tug my head back into a kiss. With some willpower I didn't know I possessed, I refuse for the moment. "I liked what you told me in the cave. I liked everything you said to me."

A flush of pride. My virgin mate, but she likes how I make her come with just my words. And I can do so much better with my body, I promise us both silently.

"Then I'll give you everything I have, and if you don't like something, you'll tell me so, right?" I press, squeezing her hips as I ask.

Her mouth falls open at even that slight pressure, but she nods, so I reward her with the kiss she wanted, moving my hand from her hip to her hair, holding her to me and kissing her until I can feel her go slack against me, knees weak as she leans in for more.

"Good girl," I murmur against her lips, separating to let her get a breath. I return my attention to her neck, looking for every spot that makes her gasp or moan.

Leana's hands find my chest, her little fingernails digging into my skin, delicious pinpricks that almost drive me to distraction. But no, she won't distract me from my mission.

I imagined this moment a thousand times when I was locked up. Guiltily, desperately, even angrily—but none of those imaginings feel right now. Those were the dreams of a desperate, deprived dragon.

And here I am, with the greatest treasure the world has ever seen in my arms. No longer deprived, perhaps, but certainly still desperate.

I debate what to do next, how best to make her come apart, when her hands trail up my chest and around my neck, leaning more of her weight on me. "Osir?"

Every time she says my name, a spark inside me glows brighter until I think my fire could compete with the sun.

"Yes, treasure?"

"Take me to bed?"

I move quickly, hoisting her up by the waist and encouraging her to wrap her legs around my hips. She does, squealing when her feet first leave the ground, but then she holds me close and pulls me into another kiss.

I am hard as diamonds, and I feel her beautiful cunt pressing against me and nearly go to my knees. I need to be inside of her. But first, I need to make her come. I need to make her see stars, and I need her to cling to me, to be desperate to have me inside her.

My poor mate has believed that sex would be perfunctory at best, and possibly something quite painful. I don't blame her for that assumption; I've seen the world she lives in. But I will not do anything to her that she believes would cause her harm. I will not do anything she feels even slightly ambivalent about.

I have to prove that sex with me is worth having, and I hope I'm up to the task. It has been more than a century, after all.

I kiss along her jaw, forcing the thought from my mind. I will be everything she could have ever dreamed of. And, thanks to our time in the cave, I already have an idea of what she likes.

I'll learn everything else that makes her squirm, makes her moan, makes her gasp my name. I have a lifetime to learn it, although I plan to make a good start of it over the next few days.

I nip at her bottom lip, and her thighs squeeze tighter around my hips. I do it again, listening to her moan.

I find my bed—our bed—and lay her on it, stepping back just long enough to look at her sprawled on the sheets.

"My most precious treasure," I rasp, and I move to kneel on the edge of the bed, reaching for her tunic. "May I?"

She bites her lip but nods for me, so I start to push it up, revealing her beautiful stomach. I can't help myself, leaning down to pepper kisses on the skin as I finally get her tunic over her head.

Without looking at it, I toss it somewhere in the room for me to find and dispose of later.

"I've dreamed of this," I murmur into her belly.

Her hand lightly cradles my head, and I press kisses on her skin as a reward, slowly working my way up to her breasts.

I have dreamed of her breasts plenty. Seeing them in the cave was life-changing.

I want one in my mouth. I remember what I told her in the cave, when I was given the privilege of watching the first time she ever touched herself. I told her to go slow. To tease herself.

I force myself to take deep breaths. It's less than helpful, with the room saturated with her scent, and all I want to do is dive into her, bury myself inside of her. But that's not what she needs.

Slow. Teasing. I can do that.

Chapter Thirty-Three

Leana

He's looking at me like he wants to eat me. He's going to devour me, I think, and I'm completely lost to him, because the idea doesn't terrify me.

It excites me.

"Osir?" I ask. This room is so large that my voice seems small in it, but his eyes snap to mine immediately.

"Yes, treasure?"

"What should I do?" I hesitantly ask. I fight not to cover my breasts with my arms, already knowing he wants to see me.

And he's been nude since he rescued me, and I've looked plenty despite reminding myself not to, so I suppose fair is fair.

That doesn't change that I don't know what to do, though. He told me what he'd like to do to me when we were in the cave, but he never said what I should do to him. And I don't want to make decisions based on the stories I've heard from other girls in the castle.

I don't want what's between us to be anything like what they've told me.

"Do?" he asks, and his hand strokes softly, languidly over my stomach. I shiver at the touch, just the tips of his fingers and the lightest pressure, but enough to make my whole body feel like I've been sleeping for years and he's woken me for the first time.

"You do whatever feels good, treasure," he continues. "Most importantly, you let me please you. If I'm not pleasing you, you direct me."

"But what will make you feel good?" I press, because this is important.

He's waited his whole life for his mate. I don't want to disappoint him.

"You do," he says, and then, without giving me time to respond, he leans his body down so he can kiss my breast.

My eyes flutter closed.

He kisses around my breast and to my nipple, and I can't help but arch my chest closer to him, thoughts of hiding from him long forgotten. "Osir," I moan, and he growls against my skin, which makes me shudder.

"So sensitive," he murmurs, and it sounds like praise. Then, without further warning, he pulls my nipple into his mouth, sucking it between his lips. "I love it when you say my name, treasure. Tell me who makes you feel this good." He bites lightly, just the barest pressure, and I arch into it.

"Oh, I—Osir!" My eyes open, looking for him, trying to see what he's doing to me.

He pulls back and grins at me, huge and toothy and very, very self-satisfied. It's a grin I haven't seen yet, another new expression to discover as I learn all the facets of his human side. It makes something in me desperate for more. Desperate for him.

I stare into his eyes and see everything he wants to do to me, and my core clenches at the thought.

"Yes, treasure?"

"More of that—please."

"Anything you want," he promises, and returns to his task.

I can't keep my eyes open, although I desperately want to watch him. But all I can do is bask in the sensations, his lips against my nipple, his teeth nipping at my skin just to make me tighten and moan.

"You're so beautiful," he whispers against my sternum. "And so sensitive. Just wait, treasure—this is just the beginning."

Before I can ask him what he means by that, his hands gently tug on my trousers. "Yes?" he checks, and I nod.

He's already seen me undressed, I remind myself. Not only that: he's seen me undressed, with my legs spread, with my own fingers pleasuring myself.

And he seemed to like it a lot. So surely he's not going to suddenly see something he hates.

I lift my hips to help him, and then I am completely nude, sprawled on his bed, sinking into the softness of it as he stares at me.

"Some dragons collect art," he says abruptly.

I furrow my brow, not seeing the connection to the current moment. I want him to say something about me, to reassure me like he's so good at doing. "Oh?"

"You put every single piece of art to shame, Leana. I'd treasure a painting of you like this beyond anything else in my hoard, but I don't think I could allow someone to paint you." He looks me over, his eyes moving long and slow over every inch of me, lighting a fire under my skin as his eyes move. "But I never want to stop looking at you."

I swallow. The heat of his gaze makes me bold.

No. His adoration makes me bold, as it has for a while now. "I have a solution to that."

"Oh?"

"Look at the real thing, then."

He smiles, slow and devilish. "You'll let me look, Leana? Lay here for me to take my fill? With your legs spread for me, looking at that pretty little cunt?"

Yes. But I don't say it. "Do you just want to look?"

Is it my imagination, or are his incisors sharper than normal when he smiles? "Dragons always handle their treasures personally," he says, before trailing his hand down my stomach and around my hip, resting it on my thigh with his fingers just out of reach of where an ache is building.

He made me love my own fingers on myself. Would I love his?

Would I love more?

"Touch me," I ask, desperate to find out. With a breathless voice, I demand, "Touch me, Osir, please, I—"

He silences me with a kiss, using his body to pin me to the bed without putting any weight on me. His kiss leaves me gasping for more, pushing up to meet him.

And then his fingers trail into my folds, gently circling that spot that makes me arch off the bed, breaking the kiss with a gasp.

"Good girl," he growls against my cheek, trailing kisses along whatever part of my face he can reach while I'm thrashing around, out of control. "Chase that feeling, treasure. Just let me know what feels good."

I grab at his shoulders, desperate for something to hold on to. "This— feels— good," I gasp.

There's a rumble in his chest, one that's so reminiscent of his dragon form. "Leana, you're so good for me. So beautiful, and responsive. So perfect, my perfect treasure. Look at you, using my hand to make yourself feel good, satisfying that pretty little cunt. I want to see you come, treasure. I want to feel you leak all over my fingers. Do you want that too, treasure?"

I flush. "Please, I—please."

I don't know what I'm begging for and he knows it, but he somehow gives it to me, anyway. I'm half convinced that maybe my dragon can read parts of my mind that even I don't know, sometimes.

"Anything for you, Leana," he says, his voice getting somehow even lower. "I know what you need. I'm going to make you feel so good, treasure. Make you come until you can't see straight, until all you can think about is us."

I can already barely think about anything outside of this bed, and I don't want to.

His kisses trail down my throat, then my breasts. He stops to press a dozen kisses there before kissing down my stomach, and I laugh as he finds a ticklish spot near my belly button.

And then his mouth is right between my thighs, and his eyes flash up, as if waiting for me to react.

I bite my lip. He talked about this in the cave, and it sounded so good, but would he like it?

The heat in his eyes tells me he thinks he will.

"Please," I gasp, and that's all the encouragement he needs.

His kiss between my thighs is a type of fire I didn't know existed. Hot and slow, all-consuming as every part of me burns in the blaze he's lit. I feel wet and soft, burning as he pushes open my thighs so he can lie between them.

And then his tongue teases over the spot that makes me see stars, and I gasp, gripping the ornate wooden headboard behind me, desperate for something to hold on to before I simply float away.

He groans against my skin, and even without his words, I can hear the praise in the sound.

His tongue toys with me, teases me, pushing me to the edge of a cliff. Somehow, this feels a thousand times better than just my own fingers. I can't think of anything but him, his hands on my hips, his tongue teasing against me, his rumbling sounds sending me impossibly higher.

I gasp, simply grabbing the headboard tightly and pushing my hips up, searching for what, I don't know. All my brain can say is *more*.

More. More of him, more of his touch, more of this.

And then I find it, whatever more is, and it washes through my body like a raging, out-of-control fire.

Chapter Thirty-Four

OSIR

Her thighs tighten around my head and I double my effort, desperate to make her come on my face.

This moment, right here, makes every moment of waiting worth it. She writhes against my face, soaking me in her sweet juices, and I can think of no more perfect moment in my entire life.

She makes a sweet noise, but this time she's not begging for more. She needs relief, a moment to breathe. My poor, sweet mate, totally overwhelmed by pleasure.

She's not ready for me to send her into multiple cascading orgasms, but I'm sure with time and proper attention, I can get her there.

I pull back like she clearly wants, but not far. I want to bury my face in her forever, want the scent of her to permanently mark my skin. I have finally found perfection—I'm not going far.

She's panting still, her breasts heaving with the effort. There's a flush from her face down to her chest, and I grin against her stomach, not bothering to hide my pride.

I did that. I made her feel like that. My treasure, who now knows I will make her feel so, so good.

I can give her everything she could ever need. I can give her a castle, and jewels, and wealth beyond her imagination. I can give her a shoulder to cry on and someone to hold her when she sleeps.

And I can give her orgasms that make her toes curl. I can give her orgasms all night long.

"Did you like that, treasure?" I ask, stroking her hip absently as I talk. "Did I please you?"

"Yes, I—yes," she says, seemingly lost for further words.

I preen on the inside. "Good girl, letting me pleasure you," I murmur, watching her shiver as I praise her. "You know you're my greatest treasure, hm? And my treasure deserves to feel so, so good." I gently stroke her wet cunt with one finger, gauging her reaction. When she just shivers, I do it again. "Beautiful mate," I croon. "Can I keep going? Can I make you come again?"

"What about you?" she asks, and my too-kind queen has a genuine look of concern on her face. "I want to make you feel good."

I groan. She's too good for me, but in this case, her worry is entirely misplaced. "I am the happiest dragon in the world," I murmur. "Your cunt is delicious, Leana. Your moans are music. I want nothing more than to do this every day forever. Please, let me."

Her hand goes to my hair, stroking it from my face, and I lean into it, letting my eyes slip closed. Has she already learned how her touch can get me to give her anything?

"Flatterer," she murmurs.

"Not flattery," I disagree, pressing kisses against her thigh. Her skin is so soft under my lips, and I trail my lips higher, higher, closer to the sweet center I long for. My tongue darts out, tasting, and I shudder.

Delectable.

I bury my face in her cunt again, moaning when her thighs tighten on my head once more.

When I push just the tip of a finger into her entrance, she gasps and arches her back. "Alright?" I check. I remember our last conversation about penetration, and how she'd seemed worried. I don't blame her, and I don't want to know what she's heard before.

But this will be different.

I slowly push my finger inside of her, sucking her clit while I fill her. I distract her with lips and tongue, slowly opening her to two fingers.

I find that spot inside of her, and she practically screams my name.

It's like flying to make my mate feel like this. It feels like my first flight in a century, a high I can't possibly imagine before it actually happens, and I bask in the feeling.

I use my free hand to palm my cock, hard and desperate and just waiting for her to be ready for it. I ache, but I need her permission first.

"You have a choice," I tell her, reluctantly pulling back enough so I can speak to her. She valiantly lifts her head to look at me when I'm speaking, although her eyes seem somewhat hazy and unfocused.

"A choice?"

"Yes, treasure. Do you want me inside you? Or not yet? If this is all you want right now, I am more than happy to oblige."

I am. I will happily eat her cunt for every meal for the rest of my very long life. But I do need to be inside her to fully complete our bond.

Technically, I suppose the rule is she needs to accept my come into her body, and there are many ways to do so. I've never heard of a dragon doing so any other way than what would be expected, but it doesn't make it impossible.

"Will it hurt?" she asks me, and I ache for her.

"A moment. No more," I promise, reaching up to tilt her head to mine, hoping she can see how serious I am in my eyes. I will never hurt her. Not for anything in the world.

"Then I want you inside me," she decides.

I study her eyes for a long moment, but I have to ultimately take her word on it. My treasure is a queen, in this bed and everywhere else, and her word is law.

She's dripping wet as I slide my fingers inside her again, trying to ensure she is as open and ready for me as she can be. I hold myself above her, leaning in to kiss her as I insert a third finger.

She doesn't tense up or show any sign of pain. She's ready for me, and the thought sends something hot and aching through me.

"Are you ready, treasure?" I ask, stroking her hair from her face before moving to line myself up with her entrance.

Instinctively, she wraps her legs around my hips. "Osir," she breathes, my name a soft caress from her, and I can't hold back any longer.

Chapter Thirty-Five

LEANA

The stretch of him inside me feels like being split open, and it's all I can do to not scream.

A moment. He promised it would just be a moment. I've heard girls tell me horror stories of the ripping pain, but a moment I can handle—

His fingers return to that place he's been teasing for what feels like years now. My dragon is observant, and already knows exactly how to play with me, how to get me gasping for a completely different reason than the pain.

It's not ripping pain. It's more of an ache, and it's already fading.

"Osir," I whimper, squeezing my legs tighter around him.

My mouth falls open on a gasp. "Osir," I gasp again, his name the only word left to me. I squeeze again, and it feels like sparks being lit inside me.

He's staring at me, kneeling on the bed, cradling my body as he holds perfectly still except for the single finger still teasing me. Then he smiles, clearly realizing what my gasp means. "Treasure," he practically purrs, his whole face lighting up with a wicked grin. "Do you feel good, treasure?"

I whimper his name again, and his grin gets impossibly bigger.

I look at the man above me and want to whimper from the sight alone. Broad and strong, I can't stop the thought that this body is for me. That this strength, this beauty, this body is mine.

It's an impossible thought. A greedy thought, one I'd never even have contemplated a month ago. One I entirely blame him for, his words in my head.

He's mine, and I'm his. Mates. Bonded forever now, and I reach a hand up to touch my necklace as I squeeze around him, trying to see what will happen.

His smoldering eyes darken. "Teasing your mate," he mock-scolds, and I don't have time to ask if he's referring to bringing his attention to my necklace or squeezing around him before he slowly pushes the rest of the way inside me.

The air is punched out of me, but in the best possible way. I don't need air. I need this, this moment between us.

"Does it feel good?" I have the presence of mind to ask, wanting to know, needing to know that I'm doing for him what he does to me.

He withdraws almost entirely before pushing back in, one long, luxuriously slow thrust that makes my mouth fall open, although no sound comes out. "Does this feel good?" he repeats, incredulous. "Does your hot, wet cunt feel good?"

My cunt clenches around him at his words. "Yes," I whimper.

"Your cunt is delicious," he murmurs. "Around my tongue or my cock, I don't want to be anywhere else." His thrusts pick up speed, and so does the finger on my clit. "Can I try something, treasure?"

Right now? He could try anything he wanted.

I look up into his eyes and know he's the only one I'll ever trust like this. I nod.

He moves both hands on my hips to lift me until I'm straddling his lap, and then gently pushes me down onto him.

His cock is impossibly deep inside me, and I throw my head back, mouth falling open with a moan that is mostly his name.

"Beautiful," he rasps, and he buries his face in my neck, pressing kisses there. "My beautiful mate, so pretty when she's filled with me. Do I feel good inside you, treasure? Stretching you out, hitting all those special places inside you?"

"Osir," I moan. It would be cruel if he actually wanted an answer from me. There's no hope of me actually being able to form words as he slowly rocks up into me, using his hands on my hips to push himself deeper and deeper inside me, invading every inch of space, touching places I never knew were so desperate for his touch.

He chuckles against my throat. "Keep saying my name," he murmurs. "That's my good girl. My treasure, my mate—letting me love you like this. Are you close, Leana?"

I think I am. I can't answer in words, so I try to rock my hips myself, trying to push myself closer.

"Good girl," he groans, and he snaps his hips up to meet my thrusts. "I'm going to fill you, Leana. I'm going to fill you and make you mine forever."

I'm already his forever, I want to say. I've been his since the cave. I'm his and he's mine, but just when I open my mouth to say it, the feeling of ecstasy crashes over me, lighting up every inch of my skin, and all I can do is moan his name.

Osir's grip on my hips tightens, and then his thrusts grow sharper, more erratic before he roars my name, and I feel his hot, sticky come pour into me.

And pour and pour. I never expected it to be so much, but I feel absolutely full of it when he carefully pulls out of me.

He wraps his arms around me and tugs so I'm cradled to his chest, both of us now lying down. "Are you okay?"

The concern in his voice is touching, and I reach up to stroke his face, gently running my fingertips along his jaw. "I didn't know it could feel like that."

"Like what?"

I consider it for a moment, but I know what the only possible answer is. "Like you treasure me," I say finally. "Like it's special. Like I'm precious."

"You are the most precious thing in the world to me," he says solemnly, and I can't help but smile, turning into his chest and letting him hold me.

Chapter Thirty-Six

OSIR

I scrub Leana's body with the softest cloth I can find, using a bath soap I fret over for nearly fifteen minutes before Leana gets into the tub of then-tepid water, reminding me tartly that she doesn't need such luxuries.

I carefully re-heat the water and choose a soap with a fragrance that I think compliments her gentle nature, and choose to refrain from commenting back about the luxuries. She might think she doesn't need them, but she deserves all I can give her and more, and I will someday make her see that.

This isn't our first bath since I brought us to our room, but every other time has been a quick dip to wash away come and sweat, usually hastily squeezed in between feeding each other quick meals and the next bout of sex. But now, our time alone is about to end, and I need to remind my mate that she's a queen.

Only when she believes it will she be able to convince everyone else, and I will settle for nothing less than seeing her on a throne next to mine.

And that means ensuring that she gets a proper bath, first and foremost.

"I can wash myself," she reminds me for the third time since I've started.

"You could, but why would you? That's what I'm for."

"So do I get to wash you?"

"Do you want to?" I could certainly agree to that, her hands on my body. My cock stirs, and I hope she doesn't notice.

Without much effort, I have managed to convince Leana that sex between us can be both beautiful and very fulfilling, but I need us both to stay focused on the goal. Namely, finally having her join me in her proper place as a ruler of this kingdom.

Later, though, she can scrub me, touch me, grope me, however she chooses.

"It seems only fair," she says, completely ignorant of my current thought process.

I finish on her arm and hand her the cloth. "Whatever my treasure wants," I tell her. "But leave me enough time to wash your hair."

"Are we on a schedule today, then?" she asks, cleaning me with movements I recognize as efficient and purposeful, but my body nevertheless sees as provocation.

It takes me a moment to gather my thoughts. "Lunch," I manage to say. "If they keep things like the old days, then the council will meet over lunch." Lunch and any such marker of time has meant nothing to us for the past few days.

Returning to a world outside her perfect body, her sweet moans, her tight cunt will take some adjusting, and I can't say I'm eager for it. If I didn't need the world to know that she is a queen the same way I do, then I'd likely bar the door and demand more time for the two of us.

But the oracle was very clear to me a century ago; one day, I would know true power. It would not be my power.

Leana, the brightest star in the sky, needs her chance to shine. I am eager to live under her reign.

**

The dress someone found for Leana almost fits perfectly. It's a deep, emerald green, made out of a satin that catches the light every time she moves. The skirt is clearly more voluminous than she's used to, and it likely doesn't help that the measurements are just slightly off. She looks divine in anything, of course. But I make a mental note to make time to bring her to a seamstress so she can have a wardrobe of her own.

As much as I've enjoyed three days of nudity, she'll need clothes worthy of her for when we're in public.

"Are you ready?" I ask her, smoothing out a wrinkle in my own shirt. I need a trip to a seamstress too, given my clothes are a century out of style from what I've seen around the castle.

"Are you sure you want to do this?" she asks me, fidgeting with her left sleeve. "I'm a servant, Osir. I clean floors and change linens. I can cook a bit. But I can't lead a kingdom."

"And I'm the mad king with a reputation for murder, a century out of the world," I point out. "And Noctere is Noctere. Between the three of us, I think we will be able to manage." I take her hands in mine, bringing them both to my mouth to press kisses to the back of her hands. "Treasure, you are more suited to this than any of us. I am fully confident in that. You'll see soon enough."

I reluctantly drop her hands, and then open our bedroom door, gesturing her out in front of me.

As we draw closer to the council room, Leana squares her shoulders, lifting her chin. Something flinty comes over her eyes.

She's a queen, and she knows it, and my heart couldn't be prouder.

I squeeze her hand and push open the door.

Ganius, Lorcate, and Noctere are all already seated. I'd usually avoid being late—I was always the timely, practical brother when my brothers and I held the crown—but I suppose an allowance might be made.

Kingdom business simply pales in comparison to my lovely mate.

The room is silent for a moment, but to my surprise, Noctere speaks first.

"Leana. You're okay." The relief in his voice is palpable, and the way he clamors to his feet only emphasizes it. I feel Leana withdraw into my side, as if she plans to hide behind me.

If she means to, then I will protect her more than gladly. I will stand between her and any danger, whether it is something like that Ashar prince or my own nephew.

I watch, trying to get an idea of how she wishes me to proceed. But then, before my eyes, she changes, drawing herself away from me, although she leaves our hands connected. She stands fully upright and lifts her chin.

Regal, proud, even perhaps a little haughty. No one would doubt that she's a queen. Warm pride fills my blood, burning for her.

That's my queen.

"I am," she agrees, staring him down. "No thanks to you."

He's silent for a moment, mouth hanging open like a dead fish, but then he inclines his head. "I deserve that."

"Yes," she agrees, her voice purposefully bland.

I think of her not a month ago, visiting me in my prison. I think of how every sentence ended with my title. How bound by her duty she felt.

But I knew even then. I knew that she was a queen under that veneer of servility. And I cannot wait to see her first act as our queen.

Chapter Thirty-Seven

Leana

Whatever Osir keeps saying to me—and he has called me queen plenty in these past few days—I know I don't belong at this table.

I'm not a long-lost princess or secret royalty. I'm not an educated courtier or someone with a particular skill that would benefit the kingdom.

I'm just me. I'm not stupid, and I understand that agreeing to be Osir's mate meant that my life would change forever. I would never scrub floors again; he wouldn't stand for it. I would sleep in a bed that feels more like a cloud than a bed. The bath I use will always be hot, and inside, and big enough for both of us. And I've eaten more in the last few days than I ever have before, even with us repeatedly getting distracted.

I flush slightly. Distracted. What a silly euphemism for what we did.

Even knowing all that, I don't feel like I deserve to be at this table. What do I have to give?

Then Osir purposefully piles food on my plate, and I remember. Dragons feed their mates and accept food from their mates to accept that bond. I am the mate of a dragon king. And I will act like it.

I eat a few bites and put some food on Osir's plate in turn, which he happily and quickly eats.

I'm quiet, just listening to the goings-on of the kingdom until Ganius gives a report on the war, and specifically mentions the human magic users sent to the front.

The room goes uncomfortably still, and I know all eyes turn to me. "This kingdom needs to change how humans are treated in its borders," I simply say, because if there is only one thing I know, it is this.

I don't know how to address the king of Ashar when he comes in a few days for treaty negotiations. I don't know how taxes work. I don't know how to ensure a kingdom is fed for the winter. But I do know people, and I know the way this kingdom has treated human workers is despicable.

The female dragon, Lorcate, clears her throat. "Begging your pardon, but that's not the point of today's meeting."

Osir, to my surprise, doesn't say anything; rather, he just squeezes my hand beneath the table.

I firm my resolve. "It's the point now," I say, with as much iron in my voice as I can muster. "This kingdom just lost a whole host of humans again, thanks to dragons' actions. Dragons might be stronger, but humans outnumber you ten to one."

"But dragons are stronger," Noctere repeats, and I bristle a bit at his tone.

"So we force obedience?" I demand. "People should live in fear? Is that how we run a kingdom? Because perhaps dragons are stronger right now. And I know there aren't many human magic users. But there will be more eventually, and I can't see them remaining complacent in this system."

"She's not wrong," Ganius sighs. "History tells us the tide will turn against us eventually. A hundred years ago there were enough human magic users to be a threat to us, perhaps. I don't know when we'll reach that number again, but it's bound to happen eventually."

"So fix it now," I urge them.

The room is silent for a moment, and Osir squeezes my hand beneath the table once more. I do my best not to look at him, to keep staring the others down.

I am not Osir's puppet. I doubt he would ever even think to advocate on behalf of the humans around the castle, except for me, of course.

If they want a queen, then I will be one. And this will be my cause.

I stare them down until, at last, Noctere inclines his head. "Tell us what you envision."

***

When at last we adjourn for the day, nothing has been agreed on. But everyone listened to me, and I suppose that is all I can ask for.

I spoke for hours, with Osir continuously refilling a water glass and pushing it insistently into my hands. I felt his eyes on me the entire time, hanging on my every word, and I know I have convinced at least one of them.

Perhaps he's right. Perhaps I can do this, can be a queen at his side. I can learn about taxes and war. Right now, I know what I want to fight for.

"You're wonderful, treasure," he murmurs into my ear, bending close to press a kiss to my cheek. "As brilliant as I knew you'd be." He sucks on my earlobe, and I shiver, torn between reminding him we have an audience and completely ignoring them. I want to give into him, give into this ever-simmering lust between us. We haven't stopped touching since he rescued me from Frost, and I'm beginning to think that hand-holding is simply not enough.

Noctere clears his throat behind us. I close my eyes, intent on ignoring him, and Osir tilts his head up just enough to make eye-contact with his nephew and growl at him, giving him a clear warning.

This time is ours now, and Noctere isn't going to ruin it.

He clears his throat again. Osir tenses against me, and I can hear his breathing deepen with anger. I have half a moment to wonder if I'm going to prevent Osir from pummeling his nephew and our supposed co-ruler, or if I'm simply going to let it happen, before Noctere speaks. "Leana. Can I have a moment?"

"She doesn't have any moments for you," Osir snaps, and his hands find my hips, thumbs moving slowly, teasingly, sending sparks along my skin even through the fabric of my dress.

"I think she can decide for herself if she wants to listen to my apology or not," Noctere says, with more backbone than I have ever heard from him.

I stop and turn away from Osir, considering. Noctere stands there wide-eyed, hands spread in front of him as if he's trying to show he means no harm. I sigh.

"Give me a moment?" I ask Osir.

He huffs, but I know he's going to listen to me. Somehow, he always does.

"I will be right outside," he promises me, then leans down to kiss me senseless. It's as if he thinks he needs to remind me why I would want to finish this conversation quickly. As if I could ever need a reminder.

I grab at him, hands on his back, and pull him closer to me, like I can somehow permanently close the distance between our two bodies and meld us into one.

Noctere clears his throat again, and Osir tenses under my hands.

I peck Osir on the lips, and the tension immediately leaves him. "I'll be right outside," he promises me again, and with one last glare at Noctere, he leaves.

"Can we sit?" Noctere asks.

Nothing good has come from conversations between the two of us recently, but I nod anyway.

I watch him as I sit, careful of the voluminous skirt. How does he see me, sitting here across from him at this table? I've defied him, I've lectured him, and it could be said that I've been instrumental in him losing sole claim to his throne. I wouldn't be surprised if the spoiled prince resented me.

He won't hurt me, of that much I'm confident. Osir is just outside the door, and even if he wasn't, I think Noctere might be a little scared of me now, after what he's seen.

"I'm sorry," he says simply, sitting across from me, and cutting clear through my thoughts.

"You're sorry?" I ask to check if I heard correctly, but he seems to take it as a recrimination. Maybe I sound harsher than I intended.

Maybe he's just scared of me now.

"I was awful to you. I knew what I was asking you. What I was threatening you with. And I wasn't lying; when you came back, I wanted to give you a title, land, riches... everything."

"You mean if I came back," I say firmly.

He bows his head, chastised. "If," he acknowledges. "And that terrifies me. I want you to know, I know I've failed you, let you down. But I still think of you as a friend, Leana. But I was so blindsided. It's chess, Leana. Use all the pieces to win." He looks away from me for the first time. "Just like my father taught me. Anything to win."

"This was real life," I can't help but remind him.

"I still don't know how to fight a war without sacrificing pieces. People. And I didn't ask for a war."

No, I suppose he didn't. He didn't ask for both his parents to die at the same time, leaving him young, inexperienced, and having to be king during an oncoming war. If I'm struggling to learn how to adapt to a throne, then he must be as well.

"It's not just me you hurt," I remind him, because he sent magic users with negligible power to the front lines. I still don't know if any of them survived.

His shoulders slump. "I know. If I support the initiatives you want to make for humans, will that help?"

I look at him, really considering him. My old friend, the selfish, spoiled boy who threw deadly temper tantrums with no one around to bother to teach him to stop. Who nearly killed me.

But he's radiating sincerity. I can feel it, deep in my bones.

I look into his eyes and see it as a flash. Him, Osir, and I at this very table. The dress I'm wearing looks ridiculously extravagant, and I think Osir is stroking my thigh through the fabric. But what really captures my attention is Noctere, leaning forward in his seat, fully engaged in conversation with a human sitting opposite us.

Just like that, the image disappears. I know what I saw, though.

"It will help," I decide. "But it's not going to be easy."

"I doubt any of this will be. But the three of us—do you think we could make it work?"

Another flash, just a fleeting second this time. Three thrones. Three crowns.

"We'll make it work."

He manages a small smile for me, his brow relaxing. "Good. To tell you the truth, Osir made it very clear that me being a part of this at all was entirely dependent on you. If you tell him to kill me, I don't doubt he would."

I don't doubt it either, but I'd never say it.

"If you keep helping me with the humans in our kingdom, then we'll work just fine together," I tell him.

Maybe we could even be friends. For real this time, and not with me as his assigned plaything, the girl who wasn't allowed to disagree with him.

Perhaps he's also thinking of our childhood, because he says, "I suppose I also owe you an apology for what happened. For your mother leaving."

I cut him off with a shake of the head. "You were a child, and you made a mistake. Someone should have taught you better, but not punished you by taking away your mother. That was her choice, not your fault."

"And your mother?" he presses, seemingly determined to have it all out today.

My mother? I haven't seen her since she left, and as cruel as it was, I didn't doubt when Noctere said she didn't ask for me. "She didn't want me badly enough to keep me," I tell him. "That's not your fault either."

"She's still alive," he says. "If you want to see her."

I don't ask where she is, where she and his mother hid all these years. I don't want to know. Not yet.

"Maybe someday," I decide, but the truth is I don't know if that someday will ever come.

I don't need her to be my family, I think hazily. I have a family right here.

Chapter Thirty-Eight

OSIR

I feel like I've waited an eternity for my treasure to emerge, and I spend the entire time cursing my nephew.

I can hear their conversation, so I can't even blame him for upsetting her. But Leana giving him her time instead of me makes my teeth gnash.

I should, supposedly, handle this better with time. Although I will always guard her and her attention jealously—I wouldn't be a dragon if I didn't—I should become better at managing these feelings. But right now, I just want her back in my arms again.

When she does emerge, she looks settled. At peace, maybe. She looks like such a queen that I fight the urge to go to my knees and pledge fealty to her right here in this corridor.

Let that be something I do back in our bedroom, where she can properly appreciate me on my knees for her.

Instead, I take her hand, raising it to kiss her knuckles. "Everything is alright?" I check.

Instead of answering, she looks furtively around and asks, "In all your research about human magic users, did you ever read about any of them developing new talents after childhood?"

"No, that's completely atypical, and I can't pinpoint a single recorded case. Why?" I ask, turning my focus from research back to her, registering that she likely hasn't asked me a purely academic question.

"Because I think I'm seeing the future."

Seeing the future. My mate sees the future, a magical gift I've never heard about in a single human before. I can't think of anything to say, just staring at her in complete shock.

"It's like what I saw in the mirror," she continues, either ignoring or not noticing my wide-eyed staring.

"What you saw in the mirror?" I echo. This is new information to me, although I suppose we haven't exactly taken the time to discuss her kidnapping, what with everything else distracting us. "You looked? What did you see?"

She smiles softly. "I saw our future."

Our future? Did she see what I saw? Does she know that she is likely the most powerful being any of us will ever encounter? "What specifically did you see?"

She blushes and ducks her head. "Not here."

Not here? Then she didn't see her own fire.

I saw her and I taking back this kingdom, and I know it's come true, thanks to our combined force. The strength of our mating bond is unparalleled, and I hope I have learned to use this power for good, and to leave my selfish pursuit of it behind.

What on earth did she see?

What did she see that would make her blush?

I lift her straight off the ground, carrying her in my arms as I hastily bring us back to our rooms. Not here? Well, alright. I didn't want to be out in public anyway, not when I could have her all to myself.

She throws her arms around my neck, as if she needs to worry about holding on. As if I'd ever risk dropping her. But I'll never tell her not to grab at me, and I revel in her touch as I hurry us back to our room.

I shut the door behind us and sit on an armchair, carefully positioning her in my lap so I don't need to stop touching her for even a moment.

"What did you see?" I ask her, burying my face in her neck.

Any other time, the academic interest in what she saw would force all other thoughts from my mind. She's one of the few people in history to even look in that mirror, and she saw something clearly different than I did. She's seeing visions now.

I should be focused on that. I should perhaps be worried about that. But instead, all I can think is how good she smells, running my nose along her skin, making her shiver under my touch.

"I saw us," she admits, voice a little breathy from my ministrations. "I saw that first night, when you brought me back here."

I want to move lower on her body, tease the delicate bit of cleavage revealed by the dress, and find her soft skin under all this fabric. But her words pull me out of my haze, and I reluctantly pull back enough to look at her.

"You saw us here?" I confirm. She saw us in our bed?

What we did was magical, and I'd never deny that, but I don't think it's the type of power that the mirror shows.

"I asked the mirror to show me if we would survive, and get a chance to be together," she shrugs. "And it showed me us. In bed."

I can't help but smile, although my mind is racing with the implications of her asking the mirror and the damned mirror showing her something different than it has ever shown anyone else before. In all my research, and in my personal experience, the mirror shows people the path to power. There should not be another option.

But leave it to my mate, my treasure. Of course, Leana is the exception.

"Did it show you something good?" I ask, much more interested in seeing if she blushes again than talking about the mirror.

She doesn't disappoint, blushing and trying to duck her head, but I grip her chin lightly and tilt her head so she's looking me in the eye.

"I saw you between my thighs. Or I didn't see that, I suppose, but it was implied. And then I came, and you were resting your head on my stomach, and we just looked happy."

"I was very happy. And I'd be very happy to do it again." I lean forward, chasing her lips, but she pushes at my chest.

"I'm serious though," she murmurs, her hands still on my chest, absently stroking now. "I saw that in the mirror, before I destroyed it. But now I'm still seeing them. Since I touched the broken pieces of the mirror."

"What do you see?" I ask, because that seems much more manageable than working out the exact implications of Leana absorbing the powers of an unreasonably powerful magical artifact.

She has a soft, almost distant smile on her face. "I've only seen good things, Osir. I see a future for us. A real future."

With her at my side? I never had a single doubt.

I move my grip from her waist to slide my hands up, running my thumbs over the sides of her breasts, teasing her through the fabric. "Then let's celebrate that future," I say.

She smiles at me, the softness of her expression turning to something sharp. "What did you have in mind?"

I can't prevent myself from asking, "Can't you see it?"

"I don't think it works like that, but... oh!" she says, looking into my eyes before turning her head away, blushing.

"What did you see?"

"You. On your knees, and..." She trails off, but that's okay. I know exactly what she saw.

"Yes, treasure," I agree, lifting her slightly so I can slide out from under her, sitting her on the chair and going to my knees in front of her. Her skirt fans out around her, and my hands immediately seek out the hem. "You saw me worshiping my mate, hm?"

"Worship?" she asks, voice growing arousingly husky.

"Queens and goddesses receive worship from supplicants on their knees," I say with as much mock-sternness in my tone as I can muster, lifting her skirt and pushing it past her knees. I still can't see what I desperately long for and curse softly to myself. "All this damned fabric."

She has the gall to laugh at me. "You were the one so insistent I deserved nicer clothes."

"I am now the one to insist that naked is my preferred choice," I retort, pushing the skirt up further.

Finally, I bare my treasure to my eyes, her glorious cunt on display. Someday some ladies' maid will teach her about the proper undergarments a queen wears under her dresses, and I will mourn that moment. But today, she is bare before me, and I waste no time leaning forward to bury my face in her delicious cunt.

She's already wet for me, and I spare half a thought to wonder if her vision made her wet. But then her soft, breathy moan lights my body aflame, and I couldn't possibly focus on anything else except making her make that noise again.

I am impatient to make her come, to taste her as she floods my mouth. All other thoughts leave my mind entirely, and the beast that is inside me, the beast that drives me to collect and possess, wants me to claim this one more thing.

Except it won't be one more thing, because I am a greedy, greedy dragon, and her soft gasps of pleasure are something I will simply never have enough of.

"Osir! Oh, oh, I—" She gets cut off by a moan, so I reluctantly slow my efforts, wanting to hear whatever she wants to say. "Osir, I want you inside me."

A very worthy thing to hear her say, then, and I fear my cock will simply burst out of my trousers at the thought. I reach down to palm myself. Soon.

"You want me inside you?" I ask, breathing against her cunt.

She squirms. "Yes!"

"You like when I fill you up, treasure?"

"Yes," she whispers, and I look up to see her head falling back, the long line of her throat on display.

"Tell me how badly," I demand, squeezing my cock at the sight of her. "Tell me how badly you want me."

She squirms, and I put my hands on her knees to ensure she keeps her legs spread for me. "What do you want, treasure?"

I wait, hoping she'll respond. Hoping she'll demand what she wants.

After a long moment, she looks down at me, biting her lip as she looks into my eyes. Then something changes about her face, and I wonder if she saw something again, some sort of vision.

"I want you inside me," she murmurs. "It feels so good when you're in me—I can feel all of you. The whole world is just us and I love it. I never knew anything could feel like that. Please, Osir."

Leana, my Leana, my treasure. Knowing she's as desperate for me as I am for her makes me nearly feral, and I can't hold off any longer.

"I'll fill you up just like you want," I promise, trailing my fingers up her bare thighs. "I'll fill you and make you scream loud enough that the whole castle will be aware their queen is being pleasured as she deserves. I'll stretch your sweet little cunt around my cock, treasure, and fill you until you're dripping. But first, I need to feel you come all over my face. I need you wet and soft and open for me, treasure."

My fingers reach the apex of her thighs, and I don't waste any time pushing two inside her and curling them to find the spot that makes her cry out. I grin against her thigh. "That's it, treasure. So fucking beautiful like this, aren't you?" I lick through her folds, pulling back just enough to say, "Come on my face, mate. Mark me as yours. And then I'll fill you, I promise."

I lick her swollen clit, swirling my tongue around it while I push my fingers deeper inside her, opening her for me. We've fucked a great deal over these last few days, but I won't risk hurting her by going too fast. No, I'll make her come on my face, make her soft and wet before I push inside her, just like I promised her I'd do when we were in my prison.

Between my tongue and my fingers, she's lost the words to respond to me. She humps against my face, and her little cunt squeezes around my fingers, desperate for them.

Yes, my treasure, absolutely perfect, look at how badly she wants me—

"Osir!" she gasps, and her walls clamp around my fingers as her orgasm takes her.

I lap at her come, desperately tasting her. I don't yet know how to convince her that I want her to come on my tongue at least five times a day, but I'm sure I'll find a way.

I'm addicted to her taste, licking it off my lips as I pull away from her, refusing to waste a single drop. I look up at her, gratified to see her face flushed and her chest heaving.

"I want you to fuck me now," she says, her voice soft but nonetheless authoritative, and I have to push my trousers down in response.

"And I want to fuck you," I promise her, pushing back from the heaven between her legs to undress myself, throwing my clothes who-knows-where, desperate for her now, an aching, sharp need not letting me think about anything else. "How do you want me, treasure?"

"Inside me?" she says, but it sounds like a question, her authoritative voice gone.

"Inside you," I agree, naked now, standing so I'm looming over her. "Do you want it slow? Fast? In bed or right here? I'm yours, treasure. Direct me."

She doesn't answer, but she does stand, then turns. "Help me with this dress?"

I scrabble at the laces, then push the fabric down as quickly as I can. I'm sure seams rip, but I can't be bothered to care. Not when her skin is being revealed to me, gorgeous and bare.

"I want to lick every inch of you," I breathe, lips an inch from her shoulder.

She shivers, but turns back around. "You promised to be inside me."

And I don't break promises to Leana.

"You like me inside you?" I ask rhetorically, grabbing her thighs and hauling her up until she can wrap her legs around my naked waist. "I'll be so deep inside you that you won't know where you end and I begin, treasure. I'll fill every inch of you with my cock. With my come."

She whimpers, and her nails dig into my shoulders, which only spurs me on more.

Every mark she puts on me is a claim, a brand, and I lose my mind just thinking about it. I take three steps, then slam her against the wall, kissing and sucking at her neck right above the necklace that marks her as mine while I line myself up to push into her.

She gasps when I fill her, and I force myself to go still, giving her a moment to adjust. Her nails dig in deeper, and I suck a bruise into her neck.

"Did you see this in your vision?" I demand, kissing along the skin I bruised.

She gasps, then rocks experimentally against me. "Yes."

I groan. "Yes? You saw me filling my mate as demanded? You saw me pressing you against a wall, hungry for you?"

She rocks again, and I fight for control to not simply pound into her. "Yes!"

"Yes, who?" I demand, rocking her very gently, testing if she's ready for me.

"Yes, Osir!"

I lose control when she practically screams my name, grabbing her hips so I can lift her and pound into her. She shouts my name again, and my entire world narrows to just her. Her breathy shouts. Her warm cunt, holding me in its delicious grip. Her hands on my shoulders, her legs around my waist, her gorgeous throat moving in front of me with every thrust.

I lean in to suck more bruises on her neck, giving her a second necklace of my marks. "How does the vision end?"

She doesn't answer right away, so I squeeze her hips to prompt her, and she gasps, "I—I don't know! It doesn't work like that, I only see a second or two, and—"

I thrust into her hard enough that she moans, losing her train of thought. "I'll tell you how it ends, then," I growl against her skin. "I make you come, treasure. You come screaming my name loud enough for everyone in this castle to hear. And I fill you up so good you'll find me dripping out of you all night long. And then we do the same thing, over and over again, forever." I thrust into her particularly hard. "Does that sound right to you?"

Her cunt walls squeeze around my cock. She doesn't answer me with words, just her body, but the shudder that goes through her tells me she agrees.

I shift her slightly, using one arm to brace her against the wall so I have my other hand to play with her clit. I love making her lose control of her lust, but I am harder than I ever remember being in my life, and if I don't make her come soon, I worry I'll embarrass myself.

Luckily, she seems to be as close as I am, because one touch sends her screaming over that edge, my name spilling from her lips as her arms, her legs, and her cunt grip me tight.

I can't hold back a moment longer, filling her as I promised her I would, roaring my pleasure for the whole castle to hear.

"Osir," she whispers against my ear, her voice well-fucked. A bolt of pride rips through me, and if it were even remotely possible, that voice would make me hard again.

It's not possible, but I don't need to see visions to know I'll be inside her again tonight.

She rocks slightly against me. "Treasure," I groan, the exquisite pleasure and pain of so much stimulation making my knees weak. "Hold still a moment."

Her cunt squeezes around me in what I'm sure is delicious torture for us both as I walk to the bed.

I finally pull out of her as I lay her down on the bed, feeling the loss acutely. But the loss is almost soothed by the sight of her cunt, wet and open. I stare hungrily, watching my come slowly leak from her.

She squirms on the bed. "What are you doing?"

"Can't you see?"

"I told you, the visions don't seem to work like that, I only see a second or two—"

"Then I'll have to get a mirror, so you can watch this mouth-watering sight yourself."

"No more mirrors."

"An ordinary mirror," I promise her, reaching out to touch her, pushing some of my come back inside her. She keens, legs shaking as she twists. "More?" I ask her. "Or too much?"

"I... I..." She twists, but, with what seems like conscious effort, her knees fall open, letting me touch to my heart's content.

"As my queen commands," I say huskily, falling onto the bed and putting her legs over my shoulders, more than ready to give her what she wants.

CHAPTER THIRTY-NINE

LEANA

When Osir finally lets go of my legs, it takes me several long moments to get my breath back. When I do, he's curled up beside me, watching me with soft eyes.

I reach out a shaky hand to touch the corner of those eyes. It's hard to believe that this man right here, looking at me so softly, is also the dragon who can tear through a man's throat. It's equally hard to believe that he is the man who said such filthy, arousing things to me a few minutes ago.

My fingers trail down to the mess around his mouth. Maybe not so hard to believe, then, considering the evidence.

I smile. "You asked me to come on your face to mark you," I remind him.

He smiles, wide and self-satisfied. I suppose he should be—my whole body still feels like it's trembling from the force of the pleasure he gave me. "You'll have to mark me daily," he says. "Perhaps hourly."

I laugh. "Do you intend to do any actual ruling, or was that just a euphemism for taking me to bed?"

"If you think I can't rule with my mate's come on my face, then I'll gladly prove you wrong," he mock-growls at me, leaning forward to nip the top of my breast teasingly. "I'll go right now, show the kingdom just how besotted their king is, how much he pleases his queen."

He makes a move like he'll get out of bed, and I find the strength to lunge for him, laughing as he lets me pin him to the bed. His hands find my hips, helping me straddle him, and he looks up at me with naked adoration on his face.

It's a heady feeling, to be so adored, and I still don't know what to do with it. Accept it, I suppose, and return it in full.

But even so, I don't let his adoration dissuade me from my course. "You will do no such thing," I say, planting my hands on his chest in a move I hope is firm. "The sight of you like this is for me."

His smile only grows wider. "My mate is possessive," he notes, glee in his voice.

"I—I'm not possessive," I argue, but my voice falters. I've never had anything to be possessive over. I never even had parents to be possessive over, not when I knew my mother would choose her queen over me long before she was called to do so.

But what else could this feeling in my gut be described as? This raw, primal need for him, for this sight, to be mine?

"You are," he confirms, still gleeful. "Like a dragon."

"Dragons don't have the sole right to possessiveness."

"No, because my beautiful human treasure is possessive too," he agrees. "Have no fear, treasure. You have owned my heart and soul for four years now. You own my body, my orgasms. And if you want to own seeing me like this, it's yours."

He moves suddenly, so he's sitting upright, holding me close in his arms. "I am yours, Leana. For eternity."

I touch the rubies around my throat. "And I'm yours."

A deep rumbling, sounding more like it belongs to his dragon form than this one, escapes him. "Yes, treasure." He just holds me for a long moment, but then he says, "If you want to be possessive of me, Leana, there is one more thing you can do."

"Oh? Are you not already mine?" I ask, trying to sound haughty like he so clearly likes, but also worried.

Is he not already mine?

"Until the day I die, and into the next life too," he promises. "But dragons mark their mates."

I touch the rubies again. "I know."

"Dragons who mate with dragons mark their mates permanently. It's a practice skipped with human mates, but you have the fire of a dragon in your small body, Leana. You could mark me."

"How?" I ask breathlessly, already captivated by the idea.

I'd thought fleetingly of asking him to help me find some jewelry his human form could wear, a counterpoint to my necklace. But this sounds much more permanent, and much more appropriate.

I have no jewels of my own to give him. I didn't spend my life collecting treasure. But I have fire.

He takes my hand and drags my fingers over the side of his neck. "If you want to kill a dragon, you aim right here," he murmurs. "When a dragon is fully turned, it is their only weak point."

I hesitantly stroke over the red scales that are there even in this form, not liking to think about it. I don't want to know how to kill him.

"And if you burn right there, in dragon form, with enough concentrated flame, you can leave a permanent mark," he continues, as if he didn't just discuss his own death.

"Would it hurt you?"

He shrugs. "Your flames hurt me, just a little, when you burned through my manacles. But I would endure so much pain to wear your mark, treasure. Don't let a little pain deter you."

I bite my lip, not liking it, but I also can't deny the eagerness in his voice as he talks about it. "And how's it done?"

"I turn, I hold still. And you burn a mark on. So everyone who sees me knows without a shadow of a doubt that I'm yours."

"What mark?"

"That's up to you. It's your mark, Leana. And I'd be honored to wear it forevermore."

I reach for his chin, turning his face to mine and trying to look him in the eye, trying to force one of the visions.

When he looks back into my eyes, I see it, just the briefest flash. I see Osir, looking into a mirror—as he said earlier, a perfectly ordinary one—and staring at the design burned into his scales with naked, vulnerable wonder.

The vision only lasts a second. I'm starting to think of them as reflections in a mirror, a mirror that shows me the best future I can reach.

"I'd be honored," I tell Osir, moving so both hands are cupping his face and leaning in to kiss him.

He's not fooled, though. "What did you see?"

I smile. "A future where we're happy," I tell him. "And you're mine."

He smiles back. "That's the present too, treasure," he says. "But if you want to mark me for the world to see, then we need to go somewhere where I can change."

***

We end up in the garden right outside our room, both of us still naked. Osir assures me that this garden has always been private, just for his enjoyment.

"And the servants who tend it?" I challenge.

"I'll burn them alive if they come here to leer at their queen."

"You will not," I say sharply.

He concedes. "No, I wouldn't, if only because it would upset my queen. But no one else will look at you like this, treasure. I can be possessive too."

I'm more than aware. My legs still feel a little weak from his possession.

Thankfully, we are alone in the garden. I make a note to speak to the staff about appropriate times to visit this place.

Osir doesn't wait any longer, changing into his dragon form, a form so big it takes up most of the garden. In fact, it looks like it's deliberately sized for him, like someone designed this garden with a dragon in mind.

For all I know, they did, and I picture Osir lying out here in dragon form, sunning himself.

Osir doesn't waste any time presenting his neck to me, and I can see his eager anticipation in the slight quaver of his limbs.

I bring my flames to my hands. "I need your flames too, Osir," I murmur.

He turns enough to breathe on me, a small, concentrated stream directly at my hand. His fire leaps to my flames, as if overjoyed to join me.

"Hold very still," I warn him, and then begin to draw.

It takes me almost fifteen minutes, and I need him to give me more of his own fire twice. Doing so is delicate, because I don't want him to move his neck and risk ruining my design, but we make it work.

When I at last extinguish my flames, I rest my hand on his neck underneath where I just burned. The last scales I burned are still red-hot, and I watch until they cool into a stark black against the red of his scales.

"Did it hurt?" I ask him softly, gently petting the unburnt skin.

"Yes," he admits, and I would feel bad, but he immediately says, "And I would burn a thousand years to know I am yours, treasure. Your mark is worth any pain."

When the last scales stop burning, I look over my work. "Do you want to see it?"

He turns back to a human before I even finish speaking, leaving my hand hanging in mid-air. He takes off for our room, looking for the mirror in the bathing chamber.

I laugh and follow him, only to run into his back, where he's stopped stock-still, watching himself.

I'm gratified to see that the design looks just as good on his human body, just as clear and just as obvious what I intended.

"I am marked by your flames," he whispers, turning his neck slightly to watch the flame pattern move.

I wrap my arms around him from behind, leaning my weight into his back. "We're both beings of fire, Osir."

"Indeed," he agrees, reaching up to touch the mark.

Before I can check on if the pain has abated, he turns, grabbing me and moving me in front of him, so we're both facing the mirror.

We're a striking image, but I don't get to admire it long before he turns me again, pulling me into a kiss.

"My treasure," he rasps, resting his forehead against mine.

I smile, looking up into his eyes, but I don't have to see the future to know what will come next.

Chapter Forty

LEANA

"Is the crown necessary?" I ask, adjusting it yet again.

I think Osir tried to fit as many pieces of his hoard as possible onto me today. While I'm only wearing the one necklace—and I doubt any other necklace could ever compare—he has presented me with rings, bracelets, hairpins, a golden anklet, and finally this tiara.

"I think you need a reminder that you're the queen of this castle," he says sternly, sliding behind me to reposition it himself. "Queens wear crowns, and my queen deserves the finest crown I can possibly find."

I roll my eyes, which he of course sees in the mirror. "And your crown?" I ask.

He picks it up from where he abandoned it to attend to me and presents it to me, bowing his head before me. "Waiting for my queen to help me with it," he answers.

He's always so dramatic. But ever since he let me mark him, I've started letting myself give into that little possessive thrill whenever I feel it. He clearly has no objections.

And right now, with his head bowed before me, waiting for me to crown him, I feel that little thrill inside me.

He's mine. He's a king. He's a dragon. He's competent and deadly and also entirely, completely mine.

I don't resist the urge to kiss him either, pulling him into a kiss that leaves both our crowns slightly crooked.

He frowns and fixes mine again, then smoothes the voluminous fabric of my dress where his grasping hands mussed it. "I love the world knowing you're mine, treasure, but not like that," he murmurs.

I adjust his crown. "Everyone knows I'm yours."

"And I'm yours, my queen. Are you ready for this?"

He offers me his arm, and I smile as I take it, letting him lead me out of our room.

Something shifts outside of our space, and we have to become the people who rule a kingdom. I can't say I hate it; as unqualified as I felt for this role when Osir first insisted I'd be his queen, I have to acknowledge that I like the results.

There are human servants in the halls as we pass, and I'd like to think they're more at ease than they were under Braxil's rule. Their conditions have improved greatly, but I'm not done pushing for more for humans across the kingdom.

I'm proud of my success, and I've had the support from my mate and Noctere—who I might even tentatively call a friend again—that I was promised.

Today will be the first time I truly test my capabilities as a ruler.

Osir pauses partway down the hall, then leans down and kisses my temple, like he can read the worry on my mind.

"Don't be nervous," he murmurs. "You will be fantastic, treasure."

"We'll see."

"I know," he disagrees. "This treaty with Ashar will be easy, Leana."

I smile at his confidence. "I'll follow your lead."

He shrugs. "For today, maybe. But I know you have thoughts. And I expect you to make them heard." He pauses for a second. "And if you see something that could be helpful to us..."

I nod. "I'll find a way to let you know." The visions haven't stopped, and I already plan to look into the king's eyes to help us work out the best possible future.

But I look up into Osir's eyes and get the briefest flash of the future, a momentary glimpse into tonight.

I flush, and he laughs, repositioning my arm in the crook of his elbow. "I doubt that had anything to do with negotiations today."

"I'm assuming it means we'll both be happy with how they go. Happy enough to celebrate tonight," I return.

"Oh, I already knew that would happen, without needing to see the future. I have plans, treasure."

"Will you tell me, then?"

He laughs softly. "I'll tell you I plan to have you wet and dripping for me all night long. The rest, you can wait for."

He stops us again, right outside the room where our meeting will be held. Noctere is already waiting for us.

Noctere stands straight, shoulders back, eyes forward, with a downward quirk of his lips the only hint he heard Osir. He looks far more kingly than he ever did before. The blustering and desperation is gone, and now I know the three of us will present a united front today.

Noctere nods at us, then turns to the door, pushing it open. A herald announces him, and I go to follow, but Osir stops me. "Most important person goes last," he murmurs, removing my hand from his elbow and kissing my fingers before dropping my hand and turning to enter the room.

Left standing alone, I take a deep breath, squaring my shoulders. I feel the weight of the rubies around my neck and the crown on my head, and then enter.

"Her majesty, Queen Leana," the herald says.

I keep my head high and go straight for the throne waiting for me, right between Osir and Noctere. When I get there,

I settle into my throne with minimal fussing with the ridiculous skirt, then look straight ahead.

The king of Ashar and his surviving brother are here, and I aim to walk out of here with a peace treaty, and perhaps an agreement for how humans should be treated between the two kingdoms.

I reach over and take Osir's hand, squeezing it once gently. Then I look over the room once more and nod.

It's time to begin.

LOOKING FOR MORE?

Receive an exclusive spicy bonus scene about Leana and Osir by signing up for my newsletter at addyjameswriter.com!

ALSO BY

Supernatural Christmas

A Werewolf for Christmas

A Recipe for Love

Crae Romance

Callum

Bryce

Heath

Celia

Silas

Estrid

Standalones

The Heat Cure

ABOUT THE AUTHOR

Addison James is a romance book author from New England. They are obsessed with all things mythical, mystical, and magical. A lifelong fantasy reader, that evolved to fantasy romance as they grew up. Addison always has a story to tell and is excited to introduce you to their world of fantasy romance. Addison can be reached through Tiktok, Instagram, or Threads (@Addyjameswriter), through email at addyjames@addyjameswriter.com, or through their website, www.addyjameswriter.com.

www.ingramcontent.com/pod-product-compliance
Lightning Source LLC
Chambersburg PA
CBHW021459110726
47899CB00001BA/218

* 9 7 9 8 9 9 2 4 4 5 2 6 8 *